ABOUT THIS BOOK

In this sequel to *Fate, Love & Loyalty*, a mountain lion shifter's family is reunited—and her loyalties divided.

After a shifter cat fight in the middle of town two years ago, Aster McCabe and her sister, Reeve, were banished from Havenwood Falls. All memories of their hometown removed by a protective spell, the sisters have lived a settled life in Denver with their mates. But their world was rocked when Reeve's infant daughter is kidnapped, and just days later, their parents show up on Aster's doorstep. Parents they don't remember.

With her niece in danger and the Denver mountain lion shifter den in turmoil, Aster doesn't have time to process her restored memories of a life she had forgotten. And according to her parents and the entourage of supernatural friends they brought with them, she only has twenty-eight days before she loses those memories again. But finding her niece comes first.

The search takes the group far from Denver, and along the way, severed bonds begin to heal. As time counts down, Aster needs to decide if she wants to go back to the town that threw her out and fight for Reeve to be able to return home too, or if it's better to forget Havenwood Falls once and for all.

HAVENWOOD FALLS BOOKS

Forever Loyal by E.J. Fechenda

Fate's Demand by Emily Cyr

The Wu & the Wand by T.V. Hahn

A Demon's Redemption by JD Nelson

Also try the YA line, Havenwood Falls High; the historical paranormal line, Legends of Havenwood Falls; the darker, sexier side of town, Havenwood Falls Sin & Silk; and the local supernatural college, Sun & Moon Academy.

Stay up to date at www.HavenwoodFalls.com

BOOKS BY E.J. FECHENDA

The New Mafia Trilogy

The Beautiful People

Clean Slate

Endings & Beginnings

Enforcer (a prequel novella)

The Ghost Stories Trilogy

End of the Road

Havoc

The Triangle (Coming Soon)

Havenwood Falls

Fate, Love & Loyalty

Forever Loyal

Havenwood Falls High

Fata Morgana

Legends of Havenwood Falls

Fated Beginnings

Havenwood Falls Sin & Silk

Stray With Me

Sun & Moon Academy

Book One: Fall Semester

FOREVER LOYAL

E.J. FECHENDA

For the Havenwood Falls fandom—you inspire me with your enthusiasm and love for this magical world.

CHAPTER 1

*A*ster stared at the note in her hand, with its bent edges and worn corners from repeatedly being touched. A photo album lay open on her lap, revealing happy images of a family she didn't remember. The only person she recognized was her sister Reeve, who was currently sitting next to her on the sofa. Aster tucked a stray hair behind her ear and read the note again, even though she'd known the words by heart for almost two years now.

Our Darling Daughters,

Your memories of us will fade, but know that our thoughts are constantly of you, for we remember. We can't explain why, but know that when we are finally allowed to, we will come for you. You were banished from our lives through no fault of your own but by laws established to protect the lives of many. The laws are tough but they have their purpose. This album is a touchstone and a way to keep our faces as part of your recollection.

Please know you are loved and you aren't forgotten. Love each other—always.

Love,

Mom & Dad

Aster traced the loops on the cursive "L" and peered at the family portrait. She and her sister, Reeve, sat in the front next to a guy who apparently was their brother, Braden, based on the handwritten caption below the picture. The resemblance was there —they all had varying shades of red hair. Reeve's and Braden's were more auburn, while Aster's had an orange gold hue. Their alleged parents stood behind them. Aster could see glimpses of herself in the mother's features: the straight nose, sharp cheekbones, and clear green eyes. Reeve had inherited her heart-shaped face and the auburn hair. Sometimes it was like looking at a catalogue of strangers, but not all the time.

"Every once in a while I'll feel this tug, like something is familiar, or a smell will resonate deeper and starts to call up a memory, but it never surfaces," Aster said, looking at her sister. "Does that ever happen to you?"

Reeve nodded and plucked her breast free of her daughter's mouth. Mina had fallen asleep while feeding, her eyelids fluttering as she slipped into dreams.

"I wish we knew more. The not knowing and the mystery of it all frustrates the hell out of me. What happened? Why can't we remember anything?" Reeve set her infant down on the middle cushion between her and Aster, placing a throw pillow on the outside, toward the edge, to keep the baby from rolling over and onto the floor.

"I don't know," Aster said with a sigh and tucked the note back into the photo album before closing it. She set it on the coffee table in front of her before gently caressing her niece's chunky cheek. "At least we have each other and the den. We're our own family now."

"Damn straight. You're stuck with me." With a yawn, Reeve stood up and stretched before disappearing into the kitchen. She returned moments later with a plate of brownies and two glasses of milk. "Alice dropped these off earlier. I was going to wait until Patrick came home, but who knows how long the guys will be gone."

Reeve's mate, Patrick, was beta of the Denver den of mountain lions. Aster's mate, Gage, was the alpha. The previous alpha, Damian Stone, had been part of a purist sect that had been growing within the den. He hadn't believed in interspecies breeding. Mountain lion shifters were becoming scarcer. Determined to create a dominant line, Damian believed that the offspring of an alpha and the daughters of other alphas would ensure the survival of the species. Reeve had been abducted by Damian, yet she escaped. That was where her recollection grew hazy. For Gage, too. He had been Damian's beta at the time. When he learned of the breeding house, where Damian kept a half dozen daughters of alphas captive as his personal breeding harem, Gage went after Damian, who was tracking an escapee: Reeve.

Gage remembers killing Damian in a vicious battle, just not where. Aster returned to Denver with her mate. Reeve and Patrick had come with them, too. Damian's corpse had arrived ahead of them, and he was laid to rest. His funeral turned into a ceremony where Gage assumed leadership.

It had been almost two years since Gage became alpha, and every day had been a battle to remove the members who were purists and had been poisoned by Damian's rhetoric.

Aster and Reeve spent many a night together while their mates were off dealing with issues. This was one of those nights. They put on a movie and ate brownies until Aster could barely keep her eyes open. Reeve tucked Mina into her crib, and the sisters called it a night.

Aster sluggishly made her way to the guest bedroom. Her legs felt like they were made of liquid concrete, each step a struggle. The room spun as she collapsed onto the bed. Awareness that something was wrong briefly flared right before sleep dragged her under—a warm, dark blanket snuffing out any thought.

She awoke the next morning, struggling to regain consciousness as Reeve's screams ricocheted through the townhouse, bouncing off every wall. Following the cries, Aster stumbled into the nursery to find her sister on her knees before the crib, hysterical and inconsolable. The crib was empty. Mina was gone.

CHAPTER 2

*M*ike McCabe's cell phone only rang once before he snatched it off his desk and answered.

"Ryker, how are my girls?" he asked. In addition to working for Mike at McCabe & Sons Construction, Ryker Pride was a member of the SIN motorcycle club, and occasionally he had to do runs to Denver for the MC. When Ryker made these trips, Mike asked him to check in on Aster and Reeve from a distance, since he couldn't do it himself or he'd be at risk of violating the terms of their punishment. The Court of the Sun and the Moon, the governing body of the supernatural community that lived in Havenwood Falls, had ruled that Aster be banished for two years, and sadly, Reeve had been permanently banned from town. They had shifted in public, fought in public, and Reeve had exposed the town to outside danger. The laws were harsh and the punishments severe, but they had kept Havenwood Falls a haven for supernaturals for close to two hundred years, unbeknownst to their human neighbors.

"Not good, Big Mike. Some serious shit has gone down."

Mike's hand clenched tightly around the phone as fear gripped his heart. "What happened?"

Mike listened impatiently as Ryker told him he had been

working out at the Sweat Box, the gym Aster's mate owned, when he overheard two members of the Denver den talking. "Apparently your granddaughter has been abducted. Right out of Reeve and Patrick's house. Your girls were drugged. This wasn't a random kidnapping but planned."

"Fuck!" Mike slammed his fist into his desk, causing the wood to split along the grain and a pen holder to tip over, spilling pens and pencils onto the floor.

"Do you want me to do anything?" Ryker asked, his voice sounding distant, like he was underwater, as blood roared through Mike's ears. Mike looked at the calendar on the wall next to his desk and at the date circled. Only eight days remained before Aster's two-year banishment period was over. He planned on going to her then. If he approached her earlier, the consequences would be severe. Now that his granddaughter was missing, that week seemed like a lifetime.

"Stay there. I need eyes on the situation. I'll get there as soon as I can—I just need to make some arrangements." Mike ended the call. He ran a hand through his thick graying brown hair as he gathered his thoughts and prepared himself for what he needed to do. It was time to visit the Court, to beg and grovel. A child's life now hung in the balance.

Mike drove home, navigating through the winding streets of Creekwood Estates, the development his father had built. A red Land Rover was parked in the driveway, letting him know his wife, Anne, was home. She had been in the office earlier to process payroll but left at lunchtime to babysit their grandson and give their daughter-in-law a much-needed break. Jacob was five years old now and would be starting kindergarten in the fall. Until then, Kaitlyn relied on family for child care.

The house was quiet when he entered into the kitchen through the attached garage. The twins, Roxy and Remy, whom Mike and Anne had adopted, weren't home. Roxy was most likely working at Coffee Haven. Hopefully Remy was at summer school and not goofing off, or he was going to be held back a year. For being twins, they couldn't have been more opposite of each other. Their adjustment to structure at the McCabes' house and life in Havenwood Falls had been full of learning curves, and where Remy was concerned, a source of extra gray hair.

A loud squeal of laughter drew Mike's attention to the wall of windows that overlooked the backyard. Out there he saw his wife playing soccer with their grandson, who resembled his father more and more. Mike swallowed past the lump in his throat as he remembered Braden, his firstborn and only son. Braden was supposed to take over the den someday, but his life was cut short. He cleared his throat and took a deep breath before opening the French doors that led out to the deck. Anne looked up at him and smiled before she frowned, a crease forming between her eyebrows.

"What's wrong?" she asked, kicking the ball to Jacob before striding across the grass and climbing the steps. She stopped in front of him and placed her hand on his chest, over his heart. "I hear your heart racing. Are you okay? You're home way too early."

"We need to talk. It's about Aster and Reeve."

Anne's already fair skin paled. She licked her lips before they were cinched together in a tight line—a sign he knew after all their years of marriage. She was preparing for bad news, almost like her sealed lips would keep the fear at bay. After a few seconds, she nodded, and her lips parted, letting out a sharp exhale.

"I'll get Jacob settled in to watch a movie, and then we'll talk. I'll meet you in the office." Anne called their grandson, and he half ran, half skipped over to them.

"Grampa!" he cried out before wrapping his arms around Mike's legs in a big hug. Mike chuckled and scooped his grandson up in his arms, lifting him over his head as Jacob screeched with laughter. He carried the boy's wiggling body into the house and dumped him on the sofa in the television room. A few tickles left Jacob breathless, and Mike stood up, laughing along with his grandson. Anne shook her head with disapproval, but her lips twitched with amusement. Mike hated knowing the news he brought would douse any amusement. While Anne put a DVD on for Jacob, Mike walked across the hallway to his office. He stared out the window at the front lawn and flowers in full bloom. There had been a lot of snow the past winter, and everything was lush and green. He heard the door snick closed and moments later, Anne wrapped her arms around his waist and placed a kiss between his shoulder blades.

"What's going on, my mate, my love?" she asked.

Mike placed his hands over hers, enjoying her touch. He breathed in deeply. Her scent never failed to instill calm—it quieted his inner cat. From the first day they crossed paths she'd had that effect on him, which is how he knew she was his mate.

"Our granddaughter has been abducted."

"What?" He felt her tense behind him, and her voice was raised in alarm. "When? Oh my god! Honey, we have to go to them!" She started to pull away, but Mike held onto her hands, anchoring her to him.

"We will. Hear me out." He turned around in her arms and placed his hands on her hips, lowering his forehead so it was pressed against hers. "We're going to meet with the Court and petition for an early end to Aster's banishment. We'll ask them to remove Reeve's memory spell, but I doubt we can expect them to lift her banishment."

"Screw the Court!" Anne cried out, and stepped away from him. Tears streaked her flushed cheeks, and she held a hand against her stomach like she was going to be sick. "Our girls need us!"

"Don't you think I know that! But we have to do this right. We've built a life here. We have commitments. If we act rashly, we stand to lose everything."

"We've already lost so much!" Her tears turned into hiccupping sobs, and Mike watched her sag as the fight in her was replaced by renewed grief. Closing the gap between them, he pulled Anne into his arms and held her close. Slowly she calmed down, and when her sobbing stopped, he stepped back and placed a finger under her chin, tilting her head up so he could look into her swollen, watery eyes of the purest green.

"We do this together, and if we do it right, we can get our family back. Are you with me?"

"Yes, of course."

He sealed his mouth over her lips, which were salty, laced with tears. She parted her lips and welcomed his kiss. Her taste on his tongue awakened other feelings, and he growled, pulling his wife closer so she could feel the effect she was having on him. A throaty chuckle preceded a roll of her hips as she ground against his erection before she broke off the kiss.

"We save our granddaughter first, then sex, mister." She stepped out of his embrace, leaving him hanging.

"We've been together for over thirty years, and I'm as hot for you as the first time we met."

"I can see that, Big Mike," Anne said with a smirk, lowering her gaze to the bulge testing the confines of his jeans. "Call the Court and get us an appointment. I'm going to check on Jacob."

"So bossy," Mike teased, and smacked his mate on her ass before she left the room. Knowing his wife, that would be the last emotional outburst she was going to allow herself until they had succeeded with the task at hand. She'd roll her sleeves up and dig in, displaying nothing but stoicism and strength until she didn't need to be strong anymore. He loved that about her.

With a sigh, Mike crossed the room and sat down in the brown leather office chair before picking up the phone to call Elsmed directly. The Court elder and Mike's father had a long history together back when Elsmed helped his dad start McCabe & Sons Construction. He hoped that connection would work in his favor.

CHAPTER 3

*W*ith their hands joined on the table, Mike and Anne faced the Court of the Sun and the Moon. It had been an agonizing two-day wait for their meeting—two days longer their granddaughter had been missing. Lack of sleep weighed heavily on Mike's face, and he noticed the visible strain on Anne's face, too. Mike knew the fact that the Court agreed to meet with them at all, and on such short notice, was a miracle.

The reception was lukewarm, and members of the Court sat on a raised dais so they loomed over whoever had to face them, forming an intimidating front. Torches flickered on the dark wood walls, and shadows played on the mural behind the dais, making it so the painted supernatural creatures appeared to be moving.

Almost all members were present. In addition to Elsmed, who represented the Fairchild family and managed fae affairs with Teeny Weeny Tahini, who sat to his left, Saundra Beaumont, Mathilde Augustine, and Roman Bishop (all witches), Lawrence Mills, and Michaela Petran were there. The only members missing were Sheriff Ric Kasun, Odette Alverson, and the town mayor, Barbie Stuart. Addie Beaumont, who wasn't on the Court but served as their business manager of sorts, sat off to the side, taking minutes.

"What you're asking for is highly unusual," Saundra Beaumont said. She was the first to speak after Mike and Anne explained their situation.

"We don't cut sentences short. All decisions are final," Lawrence Mills added, seeming personally affronted that the McCabes had the gall to ask.

"We know, but the circumstances are extenuating," Mike countered. "Aster's temporary banishment is up five days from today. It's not like we're asking it to be shortened by a year."

"Mike has a point," Michaela spoke up. "An innocent's life is also at stake here. What if Zoey were missing, Lawrence? Elsmed, your great-great-granddaughter is just as vulnerable."

Anne gripped Mike's hand at this unexpected show of support. Michaela hadn't been on the Court when their daughters were banished. The seat for the Petran family, a family of moroi vampires, had been empty at the time.

Lawrence scowled at the mention of his granddaughter's name, and Elsmed stroked his long chin, his expression thoughtful. There were some whisperings among the members. Teeny Weeny Tahini leaned over to talk to Mathilde Augustine. Roman Bishop spoke next, his voice commanding attention.

"So you're asking that Aster's banishment end early and for the memory spell to be restored for Reeve but not end her banishment, correct?"

Before Mike and Anne could respond, the heavy wooden doors burst open. Willow Fairchild and her cousin, Paisley Underwood, marched in, followed by Harlow Augustine.

"Harlow, what are you doing here? This is a private hearing!" Mathilde Augustine admonished her granddaughter.

"And I ask the same of you, Willow." Elsmed glowered at his great-granddaughter.

"We're here to support the McCabes and help our friend," Willow replied, tossing her long silvery blond hair over her shoulder. The three women came to stand behind Mike and Anne. Willow owned Coffee Haven, where Aster was a manager before being banished. Paisley and Aster had worked together there, too. Harlow and Aster had been friends since they were little. The young Augustine witch placed a hand on Mike's shoulder and gave it a gentle squeeze.

"This is unacceptable!" Lawrence Mills sputtered, his face turning tomato red. "There are rules in place and a code of conduct. You can't just barge in here!" His pale green eyes briefly transformed into reptilian slits, indicating he was dangerously close to shifting into his dragon form. If he did shift, his dragon would burst apart the courtroom in seconds.

"Harlow?" Mathilde asked, her tone all business.

"Aster is one of my best friends, and when Ryker told me the McCabes were petitioning for an end to her banishment and the reason why—I couldn't stay away."

Mathilde pursed her lips and shook her head before letting out a heavy sigh that echoed off the chamber walls. "Fine. You can stay, but as a witness only."

Lawrence grumbled, his bushy eyebrows pulling together when he frowned, resembling a fuzzy white caterpillar perched on his forehead.

"As I was saying, before being so rudely interrupted," Roman Bishop said, looking down at Mike and Anne with disdain. "You're requesting an end to Aster's banishment and the memory spell lifted on Reeve for twenty-eight days. All of this to aid in the search for your granddaughter. Is this correct?"

"Yes," Mike answered.

"Is that all? You don't want to request anything else, since we're all here?" Roman smirked, raising a perfectly shaped eyebrow.

Anne gripped Mike's hand again, and he could feel the tension radiating off her. He returned the squeeze, hoping to convey reassurance. They knew going into this that it wouldn't be easy and that they might not walk away with the desired outcome.

"No. That's it. We know it's unreasonable to ask for Reeve's banishment to end early. All we want is to be there for our girls and to find our granddaughter."

Roman nodded, as if satisfied with his response. "Shall we discuss this further or are you ready to vote?" he asked the other Court members.

The members conferred among themselves, and Mike started tapping his foot. The thick rubber sole of his work boot squeaked slightly on the polished hardwood floors.

"There's one problem," Saundra Beaumont said. "How do you propose the memory spell is lifted? We can't do it remotely. Your girls are in Denver."

"If I may," Harlow said from behind Mike. "I plan on going to Denver to help. Addie can teach me the spell. As a member of the Luna Coven, I am fully capable."

Mike whipped around to look at Harlow. Her brown eyes met his, and she smiled.

"Ryker is waiting for us. Paisley and Orion are going to come too," she whispered before turning her attention back to the Court, where the members were furiously discussing things again. With his sensitive hearing, Mike picked up most of what they were saying. Their concerns were what type of precedent would be set if they ended a banishment early and the risk of giving Harlow the spell to restore memories. Addie was called over to confer with her grandmother, Roman, and Mathilde, who in addition to being Court members, were leaders of the Luna Coven.

"Okay," Saundra announced, staring down at Mike and Anne. "We've discussed, and the majority of us have decided in your favor. Addie will give Harlow the spell, and Aster's banishment is over effective immediately. Reeve's banishment still stands. Not all of your daughters' memories will be restored, but it will be enough for them to know who you are and some details about their life. If Aster visits Havenwood Falls, all of her memories will be restored upon her return. You will have twenty-eight days before the memory spell takes effect again for your daughters, you, and anyone going with you. Both of you will be held accountable if Reeve returns to Havenwood Falls during this time period. Do you understand?"

"Yes," they answered in unison.

"Good. While the McCabe clan isn't one of the founding families, your family has been here since the 1950s and has been essential to the growth of our town. We do what we can to help and protect our own. No one deserves to have their child taken from them. I hope you're successful with finding your granddaughter."

A rap of the gavel ended the hearing, and they were dismissed. After standing up, Anne threw herself against Mike and hugged him hard. He wrapped his arms around her and kissed the top of her head. Her auburn hair smelled like a field of wildflowers that had been soaked in sunshine. He breathed in her scent, allowing himself to relax slightly for the first time since he'd learned of their granddaughter's abduction. Peering over Anne's head, he saw Addie approaching. Releasing Anne, he turned to face the young witch whom he had watched grow up to the confident woman standing before him. Her black-framed glasses drew attention to her brown eyes.

"Harlow, do you have a minute?" Addie gestured with a tattooed arm toward the left rear corner of the room. The numerous bracelets she wore clinked together when she lowered her arm, and the two witches walked away, their heads practically touching as they spoke quietly to each other.

"I'm glad everything went well," Willow said, coming to stand next to Mike and Anne. "Sorry we barged in like that, but when Harlow told me what was going on, I was inclined to help. Paisley, too." Willow looked over at her fair-haired cousin. Bright pink streaks highlighted the white-blond strands. While the two fae were cousins by marriage only, they shared traits common among the fae, like their petite builds and flawless pale skin. When they let their glamours drop, pointy ears and longer features showed their true species.

"Harlow said you plan on going to Denver with us?" Mike asked Paisley.

"You bet! We don't know what we will find, and my healing abilities could be of use."

"Healing abilities?" Anne asked, her eyebrow raised.

"Well, you know my dad is a healer, and I inherited the same ability. I want to come along and help in any way I can. I have the time, since I'm home from college for the summer. Aster was more like an older sister to me than my manager when we worked together."

"We'll take all the help we can get, but we're going to have to leave as soon as possible. I don't want to lose any more time, and it's at least a six-hour drive to Denver," Mike said, looking impatiently at his watch.

"I have that covered, and I'll fill you in outside," Harlow said, appearing next to Mike and Anne. She was holding two sheets of transfer paper in her hands with identical designs drawn on them. Harlow rolled the papers up and stuck them in her handbag. They all walked out together, and Mike reached for his wife's hand. She smiled up at him and moved in closer, their strides matching. They were so close to seeing their daughters and one step closer to finding their granddaughter. He wasn't going to stop searching until she was found. It was after nine at night, but they were a week away from the summer solstice, and the days already seemed longer; the town stayed busy later. People were out on the town square, and the smell of garlic drifted up the street from Napoli's. No one seemed to pay any attention to the group that had just left City Hall, which had technically been closed since five o'clock.

Ryker's younger brother, Orion, was waiting for them. He sat astride a motorcycle that was all silver and chrome. Even in the late evening it gleamed like a new nickel. Orion looked a lot like his brother, with golden brown hair and brown eyes ringed with gold. Physically, he wasn't as big, but he was close, maybe an inch shy of Ryker's six feet five. His build was a little leaner. One night, Mike was out at the Dirty Knuckle having a beer and overheard chatter that Orion was an agile fighter and when paired up with his brother, they were a force to be reckoned with.

Mike could hold his own and had the battle scars to prove it, but his brawling days were over. The last fight he was in had shaken his confidence. The mountain lion shifter that took his son's life, Damian Stone, almost ended his as well. Knowing Orion and Ryker were joining the search provided some peace of mind. He had no idea what or who they were going to encounter.

Orion wore jeans, black boots, and a leather vest that was so new and stiff, it looked like it could stand up on its own. The last time Ryker had been over to the house to hang out with Roxy and Remy, he told Mike that Orion was prospecting. Remy's ears had perked up at that, and the young cougar shifter had since become obsessed with MC culture, much to Anne's dismay. Ryker had become a mentor of sorts for the twins, especially Remy, since the first time Mike introduced them.

"So what did you have to tell us?" Mike asked Harlow once they gathered in front of Orion's Harley.

Harlow looked over her shoulder first before leaning in. "I can make a portal that will take us directly to Denver. Ryker will meet us."

"Do you know where we're going to meet?"

"Yes. Ryker is just waiting for my call, and I know we have to hurry. If we meet in an hour at Smalls Falls, does that give you enough time to make arrangements and pack?" Harlow looked at everyone in the group, her eyes meeting Mike's last.

"Plenty of time. We had everything ready just in case. Our car is already packed."

"I can be ready," Paisley said. "Smalls Falls is like a fifteen-minute walk from my house."

"Paisley, since we all live in Creekwood, why don't you meet at our house, and we'll walk over together," Anne suggested, and Paisley agreed.

"Yeah, it won't take me long at all," Orion said.

"Great, see you all at Smalls Falls in an hour." Harlow fished around in her bag and pulled out a scrap of paper, which turned out to be an old receipt from Shelf Indulgence, the bookstore next to Coffee Haven. She scribbled her phone number on the back and handed it to Mike. "Call me if anything comes up."

"Good luck, you guys. I can tell you're all nervous, and it's literally making me vibrate," Willow said, and gave everyone a hug. Mike had no idea what it was like to be an empath, but if it meant feeling everyone else's emotions, he was grateful not to have that ability.

After that, they dispersed. Harlow climbed on the back of Orion's bike, and they took off with a growl, the Road King's exhaust echoing off the buildings surrounding the square. Willow and Paisley left in Willow's Subaru, which had been parked next to Anne's Land Rover. Mike drove home while Anne made phone calls from the passenger seat. They had made plans in case the Court ruled in their favor, and now it was time to put the plans in motion.

CHAPTER 4

First Anne called Nicholas Jordan. He and his mate Audrey, the twins' half sister, were going to stay at the house to keep an eye on Roxy and Remy. Next, Anne called Mike's parents, Daniel and Colleen. Mike and Anne had taken over the construction business after his parents retired, but they helped out when needed. Even though they were in their eighties, Mike's parents were blessed with good health and seemed to have more energy than a room full of kindergartners. The day-to-day operations would run smoothly in his absence.

Mike listened as his wife went over a few details. "Ryker will be with us in Denver, so split his hours between Evan Grey—he's a fairly new hire—and Ryne Calloway. The payroll system Mom implemented before you retired is still in place, so payroll shouldn't be an issue." There was a pause, and Mike heard his dad ask some questions. "Uh-huh, yes, we're doing the greenhouse expansion at Fairy Tale Florists. Everett Weston is dropping the blueprints off tomorrow. He expedited them since he's going to be out of town next month. Oh, Irene Beckett is getting a new roof, and we're doing a slight remodel up at the Farnsworth Mining Co. Mine & Museum. Those are the new jobs starting next week. Thanks again, Dad," she said, and the call ended just as Mike was pulling into the driveway. Nicholas arrived as they were getting out of the car. He carried a duffel bag in one hand as he walked up the driveway to meet them.

"Thank you for coming on such short notice," Anne said, pulling Nicholas into a hug. "Where's Audrey?"

"No problem. Audrey is working tonight at Silk, and I just got off my shift."

"Busy night?" Mike asked, clapping Nicholas on his shoulder. He was wearing basketball shorts and a tank top that showed off his sleeve tattoo. His hair was wet and looked almost black instead of the usual brown. He smelled like mild soap. The obnoxious scented body washes were too strong for shifters who had an enhanced sense of smell.

"It's picking up. It always does around the full moon." Nicholas was an EMT, and in a town with a lot of supernaturals, things often came unhinged when the moon was full. Mike had already begun to feel the effects. Even though the magic Court-issued tattoo he had helped to control those urges, he suspected that having summer solstice riding on its coattails at the end of the week was exacerbating everything.

Maneuvering around the mountain bikes, ski gear, and other equipment that lined the wall by the car, they walked into the house. Anne was already launching into instructions, which Nicholas probably already knew by now, since this wasn't his first time housesitting and watching the twins. Stepping into the kitchen from the garage, Anne flipped on the lights over the island, which reflected off the dark gray granite counter. The aroma of garlic and tomato sauce lingered in the air, and a lasagna pan sat soaking in the sink. Mike watched as Anne walked over to the refrigerator that was covered with Jacob's colorful drawings. She opened the door and started shaking her head. She chuckled and closed the door. "I thought there might be leftovers, but nope. Remy polished off over half a lasagna."

"He's a growing boy," Mike said.

"Can't blame him, Mrs. M. Your lasagna is amazing—better

than Napoli's." He winked, his blue eyes sparkling when he smiled. "It was always Braden's favorite." At the mention of their son, Nicholas's smile faded, and he looked down at the gray tile floor.

"It's okay to talk about him," Mike said. "He was your best friend. You were like brothers. I find the memories more of a comfort now. At first, they were too painful, but it's getting easier." He looked over to see Anne nodding in agreement, but her eyes were shining as she held back tears.

"It's been nice having the twins here. Our house was too empty and quiet after—" She paused, taking a deep breath. "After everything."

It was true. The first year was unbearable. Mike hardly spent any time at home. Every room, every smell, was a reminder of everything they had lost. He immersed himself into work to avoid being consumed by grief. If it wasn't for the connection with his mate, he might have shifted and run off into the woods for the rest of his days. Anne was his anchor. His strong, brave, and resilient wife kept him from falling apart and held them together. The twins came along at just the right time. The twins needed a home, and they had a home to give.

Their grocery bill went up, along with their water and electricity bills, plus there were more shoes to trip over by the door and more clutter, but the house wasn't quiet and empty anymore. When the twins had their first sibling spat, Mike remembered looking over at Anne and a smile had lit up her face. That was a sound they hadn't heard since Reeve and Aster. Suddenly there was life and normalcy in their house again. It hadn't been perfect, and the twins were still adjusting, but a lot of healing had taken place over the past eight months—for everyone. Mike wondered about Roxy's upcoming trials for the new college the Court had created. If she was accepted, she'd be leaving. Life was like that, though—full of change and adjustments.

"So the Court agreed to end Aster's sentence early. What about Reeve?" Nicholas asked.

"No. She will get some of her memories back for twenty-eight days, but her banishment still stands," Mike answered.

"Damn. Well, at least you'll get to see her. That's better than nothing."

"We'll take whatever we can get," Anne said. "Now, let me go over a few things with you."

Mike left them in the kitchen and went upstairs. The twins had taken Reeve and Aster's old bedroom. Even though they could have had separate bedrooms, they wanted to be together. They had suffered through so much, and Remy was fiercely protective of his sister. The door was shut, and there was a strip of light at the bottom. Mike knocked twice before turning the knob and pushing the door open. Roxy was stretched out on her bed wearing leggings and a long-sleeved shirt, earbuds in and nose in a book. Remy was sitting up, his back supported by a mountain of pillows. He wore khaki cargo shorts and that's it. He had a game controller in his hands and was focused on the game displayed on the flat-screen television mounted on the wall. The twins shared the same features: sandy blond hair and honey-colored eyes that were set in narrow faces. But that was where the similarities ended.

Remy had a lot of energy and was prone to angry outbursts. Roxy was very quiet and contained. She had been severely scarred and hid her body with clothes, where Remy would probably be content running wild and free with clothing optional. Remy's side of the room looked like a dumpster fire. Dirty clothes littered the carpet, and a trail led to the wicker hamper, but never actually made it inside. Wrappers from Burger Bar and Tacos for Daze had formed a mountain of foil on his bedside table.

Roxy's side of the room was immaculate. The only thing on the floor were her flip-flops next to the bed. Her hair products and makeup were arranged on top of her dresser by size. Nothing was out of order.

"What's up, Uncle Mike?" Remy asked without taking his eyes off the screen. The twins had started referring to Mike and Anne as Aunt and Uncle a few months after they moved in. They had acclimated enough and decided calling them Mr. and Mrs. McCabe was too formal. They weren't ready for Mom and Dad, either. So, Aunt and Uncle stuck.

Mike sat down on the edge of Roxy's bed. She inserted a bookmark and closed her book, setting it down on her chest to give him her full attention. "Your Aunt Anne and I are going to Denver. Tonight."

Remy set his controller down and turned on the bed to face Mike. "Tonight?"

"Yes. Harlow is going to open a portal so we don't have to drive. Ryker is going to meet us. Nicholas is already here. He and Audrey will stay and watch you guys." One of the first things Mike learned about the twins was to be as transparent as possible. They had deep trust issues and were pretty adept at figuring out when someone was lying to them.

"Ryker's going to be there? Then I'm going too." Remy slid to the edge of his bed and bent over to pick up a rumpled T-shirt off the floor.

"No. I need you here to keep an eye on things, and you have classes. School is your number one priority right now."

His shoulders slumped, and he dropped the T-shirt. A scowl on the boy's narrow face told him Remy wasn't happy, but at least he was listening. That was an improvement.

"When will you be back?" Roxy's soft voice broke through the tension and changed the subject.

"I don't know. We have to be back within twenty-eight days. I hope it doesn't take that long." The idea of his granddaughter in the possession of strangers for that long sent his inner cat into a tizzy. He felt his skin ripple beneath his clothes and struggled to suppress the urge to shift.

Roxy nodded. "The memory spell."

"Yes, exactly. Are you two going to be okay while we're gone? I know Nicholas and Audrey are looking forward to spending more time with you." The question was directed toward Remy. Mike knew Roxy would be fine. She'd go about her routine and keep a low profile. Her brother on the other hand . . . Especially with Ryker away, well, that was a different story.

"We'll be fine, Uncle Mike. Just get back safely." Roxy's golden gaze met Mike's, and he saw the concern there. These kids had already lost so much. He promised to return and meant it. He didn't want to be the source of any more turmoil in their lives. He stood up and leaned over, kissing Roxy's forehead. "We'll definitely be back before your trials for the Academy," he assured her. Then he turned around and took the two steps that separated the twins' beds. He sat down next to Remy and ruffled his long hair before wrapping an arm around his shoulders and pulling him into a partial hug that Remy tolerated for a few seconds before shrugging him off.

"Enjoy your first Midsummer's Night Terrors and stick by Nicholas and Audrey, as it can get pretty wild. We'll check in when we can. Call us if you need anything," Mike said before leaving the room. The twins had already resumed their activities like he hadn't been there at all.

Anne was coming up the stairs when he stepped out into the hall.

"I'm just going to say goodbye," she said. Before she slipped into the room, Mike placed a hand on her arm, stopping her. She looked up at him, eyebrow raised in question. He brushed a stray curl away from her cheek, tucking it behind her ear. Words passed unspoken between them. They had been married so long they knew how to read each other's cues. Anne stepped closer to him and rose on her tiptoes to kiss him. Mike's hands circled around her waist. She was a little curvier now that she was older, and after bearing three children, but he liked that—he liked her softer curves and the way her ass fit in his hands. Her hands ran up his chest and around behind his neck before they were buried in his hair. She sank against him as he devoured her mouth, sucking on her full bottom lip, eliciting a soft, breathy moan. Movement on the other side of the door caused them to break apart, both breathless, and the longing Mike saw on his mate's face matched what he was feeling.

"What was that for?" Anne asked. "Not that I'm complaining." Her lips, glossy from their kiss, lifted with a saucy grin.

"Who knows when we'll be alone again next? I was seizing the moment." As if to prove his point, the bedroom door opened and Roxy stepped out at the same time the doorbell rang. Paisley had arrived. It was time to go.

From that point on, everything was a blur. Roxy went downstairs with them to greet Nicholas. After that, Nicholas drove Anne's Land Rover and dropped them off at the trailhead that led to Smalls Falls. They piled out, and Mike lifted the rear hatch, handing bags off. Paisley had a backpack stuffed full, and Ann carried a small duffel bag and a backpack. Mike carried the larger, heavier bag. They said goodbye to Nicholas and set off. It was less than a ten-minute walk from there, and the rush of water grew louder as they approached. The light from the almost full moon lit the narrow dirt path, but none of them needed it. Shifters and fae all had enhanced senses, and seeing at night wasn't an issue.

Harlow and Orion were already there, and Orion turned upon hearing their approach, instinctively taking a step so he stood in front of Harlow. When he recognized them, he relaxed, and Mike thought he moved away but realized Harlow had shoved him out of the way.

"Orion, chill out! I'm not some damsel in distress."

"Yeah, but you're my bro's old lady, and Crusher told me to watch out for you while he's gone."

"First of all, you know I hate being called an old lady. Secondly, I'm safe, and I can handle myself." She stood with her hands on her hips. Like Anne, Harlow had changed into more practical clothes. She wore jeans, hiking boots, and a T-shirt that said *Not Today*. A hoodie was tied around her waist. Anne was wearing an almost identical outfit, except she had on a polo that had the McCabe & Sons Construction logo over her left breast.

"Hey, Pinkie," Orion said to Paisley. He tossed his head so the hair hanging over his eyes flung back. He had his hands in the back pockets of his jeans, and he stood with a cocky, aloof coolness. With his distressed jeans, black T-shirt, leather vest, and black leather boots, he captured the stereotypical bad-boy look. Mike shook his head and chuckled to himself. It didn't seem like that long ago when he behaved that way around females, before he met his mate.

Paisley scowled at him. "Pinkie?"

"Yeah." Orion reached out, tugging on a section of Paisley's hair that was dyed pink. "Pinkie."

The petite fae rolled her eyes, and suddenly the pink streaks changed to blue, startling Orion, who dropped the section of hair he was holding. He examined his fingertips for any discoloration. "That's a neat trick, Blue."

"Ugh! What is it with guys and their nicknames? Your brother calls Harlow Country Club, and my cousin's boyfriend calls her Flannels. I don't get it." After her rant, Paisley's hair transformed into a rainbow.

Orion grinned, and his golden eyes flashed with amusement at the challenge. "Oh, I could do this all night, Goldie."

"Goldie?" Paisley's face crinkled with confusion. She walked to the edge of the pond and peered over to look at her reflection in the still water. "Explain," she demanded, turning back to Orion with her hands on her hips, practically mirroring Harlow.

"Because you're the pot of gold at the end of the rainbow." Orion winked, and Harlow groaned. Mike barked out a laugh, and he noticed Anne was shaking with laughter.

"That was sooo cheesy," Harlow said and stifled a laugh. "Come on, Lover Boy, leave poor Paisley alone. Your brother is waiting for us."

"I hope we're back in time for Midsummer's Night Terrors. I gotta know how the town puts all the humans to sleep."

"Magic, obviously," Harlow said. "I hope we're back in time, too, but who knows how long we're going to be gone."

Just like that, the antics were over and the group became

focused on the task at hand. Harlow began to whisper a spell, chanting words under her breath. The wind began to stir, swirling around her and lifting her long dark hair. A faint vibration hummed beneath his feet, and Mike stared in wonder as the air before Harlow shimmered and then seemed to part, revealing a black hole that grew to the size and shape of a doorway within seconds.

"Go!" she commanded, and Orion stepped through first, followed by Paisley. Mike and Anne clasped hands and squeezed through together. Harlow came through last, closing the portal behind her.

Mike looked around at their surroundings. They were inside what appeared to be an abandoned warehouse or factory of sorts. Part of the roof was collapsed, and debris littered the cracked concrete floor. Weeds poked up through the cracks in the areas where sunlight would reach during the day. Rust-colored stains bloomed on the floor. He raised his nose in the air and sniffed. The metallic tang of blood lingered, and he suspected the stains on the floor weren't from chemicals. Broken bottles and glass from shattered windows sparkled in the moonlight.

"Where are we?" he asked, instantly on alert in the unfamiliar territory. "Why is there blood on the floor?" He surveyed the shadows, looking for any threats.

"The number one rule about the Supernatural Fight Club," Harlow said, slightly tweaking a well-known line from one of Mike's favorite movies. He understood, and it made sense. A remote location like this was the perfect spot for a fight club, especially a supernatural one. Even Havenwood Falls had a fight club that the MC hosted, though it had been years since he participated. Mike rubbed his right ear, running his finger along the divot where the top used to be. That had been bitten off by a member of the Blaekthorn wolf pack. Anne hadn't been too pleased when he came home that night covered in blood and missing half his ear.

"Seriously?" Paisley shuddered and looked around the room.

Mike noticed she stepped closer to Orion and wondered if she even realized she had subconsciously sought out his protection.

"Yup, I've fought here before," the young lion shifter said.

"You have?" Her violet eyes were wide when she turned to look at him. "Who did you fight?"

"I've fought all kinds. My last fight was against a vampire. He was hopped up on faerie blood and almost killed me. Harlow saved my ass." Orion and Harlow exchanged a glance and Mike wondered what the real story was—it was obvious something significant had happened.

"Come on. Ryker's waiting for us outside," Harlow said, signaling an end to the conversation.

"Let's go get our family back," Anne said, sliding her fingers between Mike's and tugging. They walked together, hand in hand, a united front ready to face whatever challenges came their way.

CHAPTER 5

$\mathcal{T}$he doorbell rang, and Aster looked across the room to Gage. He was standing in front of the window, arms crossed across his chest.

"He's here," he said, and turned to face the entrance to the living room. Reeve shifted from where she was sitting next to Aster on the sofa. Their hands were clenched together, and Reeve leaned against Patrick, who was sitting on her other side. She had finally stopped crying, but the blank, numb stare worried Aster. Seeing her sister shut down before her had her stomach in knots. She felt so helpless. Alice, the woman who had delivered the tainted brownies, was long gone. They had tracked her scent to a motel, and that's where it ended. If they were human, they could have gone to the police and reported the kidnapping, and an Amber alert would have been broadcast. Explaining to the cops that they suspected a group of rogue mountain lion shifters who had been exiled from their den would not go over well.

Instead, Gage had called a private investigator who handled supernatural cases. Asa Foster was a retired detective from Denver PD. He was also a bear shifter with connections to the criminal underworld as well as federal judges. The past four days had been excruciating as they waited for news on potential leads about

Mina's whereabouts. They had basically shut themselves off from the den with the exception of a few soldiers who had been with Gage from when he had been Damian's beta. Since Alice's betrayal, trust was stretched thin.

While they were eating dinner, a solemn affair since none of them had any appetites, Asa called Gage and reported he had information and that he'd be by within the hour. That was the longest hour of Aster's life. Now Asa was here, and all attention turned to the hulking man that was escorted into the living room by Thorne, one of the few members Gage trusted at the moment.

The private investigator had to duck under the entryway, and he removed his straw-colored cowboy hat, revealing a thick head of brown hair graying at the temples. He palmed the top of his hat with a giant hand, and in his other hand he carried a manila folder. He wore a faded denim shirt, Western style, that stretched across broad shoulders. The shirt was tucked into tan Carhartt jeans, and the heels of his cowboy boots thudded on the hardwood floors. Aster's attention was drawn to his belt—not the large brass buckle, but the side holster on his hip that held a handgun.

Gage crossed the room and held out his hand. Asa met him halfway, limping slightly. He tucked the manila folder under his arm to complete the handshake. The bear shifter towered over Gage, which meant he had to be at least six and a half feet tall.

"Have a seat." Gage gestured to the upholstered chairs that faced the sofa, a coffee table in the middle. Asa sat down, the chair creaking beneath his weight, and opened up the manila folder on the table, spreading a series of grainy black-and-white photographs across the polished wood surface. Aster liked that he was getting right down to business, and she leaned forward to look at the images. Despite the poor quality, she recognized the one woman: Alice. She was holding a bundle in her arms, carrying it like one would carry a baby.

Patrick snatched up another image, his nostrils flaring. "Son of a bitch!" He handed the picture over to Gage. "See who she's with? Confirms exactly what we thought."

Gage studied the picture, and Aster noticed his hand shaking. Claws sprung from the ends of his fingers as his hand started to transform, slicing through the photo paper. He took a few deep breaths, and the claws receded.

"When was this taken?" he asked Asa.

"Three days ago, the day after your niece was abducted. They probably didn't realize the motel was under surveillance as part of a prostitution sting operation. A friend on the force let me review the footage. Your suspicions about Eben Brant are correct."

Aster sat up at the mention of that name. Eben was a purist. Part of Damian Stone's cult. He had been banished from the den almost two years earlier, after losing a challenge to Gage. She thought he had licked his wounds and moved on. She was wrong. Eben must have had Alice and who knew who else working for him from the inside. Spying, plotting, and taking revenge on the den's most vulnerable member: Mina.

"The Suburban they're seen getting into is registered to Eben. It was found abandoned yesterday, outside of Buena Vista. They torched it."

Gage pinched the bridge of his nose. "What else?"

"Coincidentally, I received a call yesterday from a small coven in Buena Vista. One of their witches was hired for some spellwork and never returned. She was only supposed to be gone half a day on Tuesday."

"Do you think this is connected?"

"I sure do. While the coven thinks a witch hunter is responsible, this witch was known for her cloaking and invisibility spells. Apparently, whoever hired her wanted to disappear."

"Eben fucking Brant." Gage stood up and started pacing, running a hand through his hair. "I should have fucking killed him!"

"Hey." Asa rose to his feet. "I don't want to hear that, so I'm going to go. What you do with the information from this point on is your business."

"No, I understand. Thanks, man." They shook hands again, and Gage walked Asa out.

Throughout this entire time, Reeve hadn't said one word. Aster glanced at her sister. She was staring so intently at the picture Gage had thrown down on the table, Aster thought her green eyes were going to burn holes through it. The picture showed Alice holding Mina, and Eben was grinning down at the baby, like a pirate who had found his long-lost treasure. Reeve's hands were curled into tight fists on her lap, the knuckles white from strain. She'd gone ghostly pale, except for hot red spots on her cheekbones. The grief that had been consuming her had been replaced—by rage.

"Patrick?" Reeve whispered.

"Yes, my love." He leaned forward and placed his hand over Reeve's fists.

"Once we get Mina back"—she pulled her gaze away from the picture and met Patrick's eyes—"he needs to die."

The cold, detached tone in Reeve's voice caused a shiver to run down Aster's spine. She agreed with her, one hundred percent, that kidnapping fucker needed to die. She knew Gage was shouldering the blame for this. He had let Eben live. He wouldn't make that mistake again.

Aster grabbed her phone off the coffee table and searched her maps app for Buena Vista. It was one of the larger towns southwest of Denver, sandwiched between the Pike and San Isabel National Forests and the Gunnison National Forest. The region was heavily forested and mountainous, which meant it offered a lot of places for mountain lion shifters to hide. If Eben did have a witch concealing their location, finding them was going to be even more difficult, and they had several days' head start. It was time to get a move on.

As soon as Gage returned to the living room, she broached the subject. Patrick and Reeve were just as eager to get started too.

"Hold on." Gage held his hand up, as they had all started speaking at once. "We can't all just rush in—we need a plan. Patrick"—Gage looked across the coffee table at his beta—"I need

you to stay here. You're going to be in charge while I'm gone."
Patrick started to protest, but Gage held his hand up again. "If
both of us are gone, things will go sideways here, and there's
already too much instability. Leadership needs to be present and
strong."

"Then you stay here! This is my daughter we're talking
about! It should be me looking for her." Patrick got into Gage's
face.

"And it's my fault she's been taken!" Gage sprung up from the
chair to pace the room. "If I had killed Eben two years ago, we
wouldn't be having this argument. It's my mess, and I have to be
the one to clean it the fuck up!" He pounded his fist against his
chest. "I did this."

"No, honey, no!" Aster went to Gage and pulled his fist away
from his chest, holding it between her hands. "You gave Eben a
chance to live and change. He chose to kidnap Mina. That's all
him, not you."

"That's not how the den will see it. They'll see it as a
weakness." He crossed the room to stare out the window. "I'm
speaking as your alpha, bro. You need to stay here."

"Fuck you!" Patrick stormed out of the room, and a distraught
Reeve followed him. Moments later, Aster heard the front door
slam closed.

"Fuck!" Gage strode past Aster, and like her sister, she
followed. He walked down the short hallway to the kitchen.

"I'm going with you," she said to his back.

He turned around to face her. "Not you, too. I'm your alpha,
and you're staying here."

Aster balled her hands into fists, feeling her claws ready to
come out. "Don't you dare pull that alpha bullshit with me! I'm
your mate. Mina is our niece, and I'm coming with you."

"Damn it, Aster!" Gage ran a hand through his hair and
exhaled sharply. "We don't have time for this. You stay here with
your sister. She needs you. Plus, you'll be safer here."

This statement made Aster see red and fired her temper right up. "Oh, it's like that, then? Let the poor weak womenfolk stay behind?"

"No. That is not what I meant." Gage pinched the bridge of his nose and growled out of frustration. "Will you just listen to me?"

"Oh, I hear you loud and clear." She turned her back on her mate, so mad she couldn't look at him anymore. Reaching into the cabinet above the coffee maker, she grabbed a glass so she could get a drink of water. Once the glass was in her hand, her plans changed. With a scream, she threw it against the wall, where it exploded into a thousand shards, which scattered on the tile floor.

"Jesus Christ! What the fuck?" Gage yelled, stepping toward her and gripping her by the shoulders.

"That's better than punching you, which is what I really want to do." She stuck her chin out. Aster knew she was acting irrationally, but there was no way she would admit it. She wasn't going to back down until Gage agreed she could go with him. If she had her way, they'd already be gone. But no, Gage had to be a stubborn ass.

Thorne coughed loudly, interrupting their argument.

"What?" they both snapped at him.

"Sorry to interrupt, Alpha, but you have visitors." He kept his head down, a display of submission—or for personal safety to avoid flying glasses.

"Who?" Gage asked.

"Crusher from the gym is here, and he's not alone. He brought a witch, a fae, his brother, and apparently Aster and Reeve's parents?"

"Is this a joke? We don't have parents." This strange arrival, so soon after Mina's kidnapping, set Aster more on edge.

"That's all I know. Should I bring them in?"

Gage nodded. "Bring them into the living room. We'll be right there."

Thorne, always quick to follow orders, left the room. Aster, who had stepped away from Gage when they were interrupted, looked over at her mate. He was pinching the bridge of his nose again and had his eyes closed. His jaw was clenched, and her keen hearing picked up the grinding of teeth. She hadn't seen him stressed like this since he first took over as alpha.

"Are you okay?" she asked.

"Yeah. No." He shook his head and opened his eyes, locking his gaze on hers. "There's just a lot going on, and I don't want to fight with you. I need you by my side."

"And I will be by your side—when we go to find Mina." Before Gage could respond, she spun on her heel, her ponytail swinging against her back from the movement. "Now, let's go see who are claiming to be my parents," she called over her shoulder. A frustrated growl followed her down the hall, and she grinned, knowing she had won.

When Aster entered the living room, she froze mid-step, her eyes locked on the middle-aged couple sitting in the two chairs that faced the entryway. The couple stopped talking and seemed just as paralyzed. Gage came up behind her and placed his hand on the small of her back.

"What's wrong?" he whispered in her ear, his breath tickling the hairs on her neck.

"It's them."

"Them who?"

"From the photo album. You know that one with family pictures of Reeve and me. That's them."

"Are you sure?"

"Positive."

The other occupants in the room had turned around from where they were sitting on the sofa to look at Aster and Gage. A woman with long black hair and Asian features sat on the lap of Crusher, whom she had met once at Gage's gym. A petite woman with white-blond hair with purple streaks sat in the middle, next to another man who looked remarkably like Crusher.

"Crusher, explain," Gage said, focusing on the one person they knew.

Crusher stood, lifting the woman who was on his lap with him and setting her down where he had been sitting. "This is going to sound really strange, but it's the truth."

"Where's Reeve? Is she okay?" the red-haired woman blurted out. She started to rise out of the chair, but Gage growled and moved in front of Aster. The man sitting next to the woman pulled her back, causing her to sob. There was something so familiar about her voice that tugged at Aster, but she couldn't place why.

"This is Mike and Anne McCabe. They're Aster and Reeve's parents and they're from a town called Hickenbocker Springs. No, that's not right. Harlem Hollow. No. What the fuck is going on?" Ryker smacked his forehead with his hand and growled.

"Babe, let me." The black-haired woman stood up and faced Aster. "There's a reason why you can't remember them—can't remember me. I'm Harlow, by the way. We were best friends growing up, and that's Paisley Underwood, who you worked with at a place called Coffee Haven." Harlow pointed to the young blond-haired woman.

"What are you playing at, Crusher? Did Eben send you here?" Gage puffed up his chest and crossed his arms, still standing in front of Aster, who was busy processing all of the new scents in the room, which were familiar too. She isolated the scent of the red-haired woman, and her heart sped up as an association was made. *Home.*

"Who the fuck is Eben? No, dude, we're here to help find Reeve's baby. I'll try to explain. You see, when someone leaves Hollywood Fields. Damn it!" He let out another frustrated growl and turned to the woman who had introduced herself as Harlow. "You better explain, Country Club. I keep forgetting that I can't.

"As I started to say, there's a reason why Ryker can't explain, and I was temporarily given the ability to talk about it—your parents, too. See, there's a memory spell in place to protect the town where you grew up. Visitors forget the town almost immediately after they leave, and residents will forget the town and any memories made there after twenty-eight days. That's why you and your sister don't remember. You've been gone for almost two years."

"Two years?" Aster placed her hand on Gage's arm. "Remember how confused we were when we arrived in Denver two years ago? The doctor thought it was some strange form of amnesia." Aster stepped around Gage to examine the visitors more closely. She saw her own eyes on the older woman's face, which was heart-shaped like Reeve's. The man had a straight nose, like Aster's, and his scent had the same association. "I need to call Reeve."

Aster pulled her cell phone out from the back pocket of her jeans and dialed. The call went right to voicemail. Cursing under her breath, she typed out an urgent text message:

911! Get over here now! Bring that family photo album.

"No offense, Crusher, but after the past few days, I'm having a hard time trusting people," Gage said.

Crusher held his giant hands up in the air, indicating he didn't take offense. "I don't blame you. I trust very few people outside of the MC and about half of them are in this room." He nodded in the direction of the visitors.

Just then, Aster's phone vibrated in her hand, startling her. She looked down at the screen to see her sister's name and immediately answered.

"Sorry, I was pumping," Reeve said. "Now what is going on? What's the emergency?"

"You know that photo album with all of the family pictures that include us?"

"Yes, of course."

"The parents in all of those pictures just showed up here."

"What?" Reeve shrieked, and Aster had to hold the phone away from her ear. "Are you messing with me?"

"I wouldn't joke about this, Reeve. They're in the living room, and I'm looking right at them. Can you and Patrick get your asses over here, like yesterday?"

Reeve sighed. "Patrick is still pissed at Gage."

"Well, he needs to get over it and get over here. Both of you do." Aster ducked out of the room and quickly walked back to the kitchen. "I'm freaking the hell out! They say they want to help find Mina."

"Mina? How do they know she's missing?" Suspicion crept into Reeve's voice.

"That's a good question. We'll ask them when you get here. Hurry, please!"

"We'll be there in less than ten minutes. Longer if I have to tie Patrick up and drag his ass there."

CHAPTER 6

*A*n awkward silence filled the room as everyone waited for Reeve and Patrick to arrive. Aster couldn't stop staring at the couple who claimed to be her parents. Deep down inside, she sensed this was the truth because of the familiarity of their scents and the physical resemblance, plus the two-year timeline matched. Or maybe it was just wishful thinking and she wanted them to be her parents, so they could fill in all the blanks.

Less than ten minutes later, Reeve and Patrick came rushing into the living room. Just as Aster did earlier, Reeve froze like a deer in headlights.

"Oh my god," she said, her eyes fixed on the older couple. She held the photo album in her right arm, and Aster pried it free of her grip. Flipping through the pages, she stopped on the most recent family portrait. She looked to be about seventeen or eighteen years old, which made Reeve nineteen or twenty. Aster examined the picture, then looked up at the couple for comparison. They appeared to be the same people. She nudged Reeve to get her attention and showed her the picture.

"How did you know Mina is missing?" Reeve blurted out, her green eyes narrowing into slits. "Is this some sick game?"

"No, honey. Not at all. We're here to help," the older woman said. "This is so much harder than I thought it would be," she said to her husband. He reached for the woman's hand and clasped it tight.

"I told them about Mina," Crusher said. "I overheard some of your members at the gym talking about what happened." He directed this last part to Gage. "Big Mike, er, Mike McCabe is my boss, and he asked me to keep an eye on his daughters whenever I'm in town for club business."

"Why?" Reeve asked.

"Because if your mom and I tried to see you or make contact with you or your sister, it would have made things so much worse," the older man answered.

"Reeve, their scents. Are they familiar to you at all?" Aster whispered in her sister's ear. She watched her sister's nostrils flare on her delicate nose, very similar to their alleged mother's nose. Reeve closed her eyes as she inhaled but they suddenly popped open, and she looked at Aster.

"So familiar. Like—"

"Home?" Reeve nodded in response.

Aster handed the photo album to Gage. "I think they're telling the truth."

Gage looked doubtful, his eyebrows knitting together when he frowned at her.

"There's one way to know for sure," Harlow said. She stood up from where she was sitting on Crusher's lap and held a rolled-up piece of paper in her hand. "The town where you grew up is protected by wards and a memory spell. Each resident has a tattoo that works like an invisible fence. It registers you as a resident and offers certain benefits. Like your memories, these tattoos disappeared. I happen to be a member of the coven that controls these wards, and I have temporary tattoos that will restore some—not all, but some—of your memories. At least you'll know these lovely people are in fact your parents. Hopefully, Aster, you'll remember that I'm your favorite best friend."

Aster turned to look at her sister, stepping closer so they could have a more private conversation. "What do you think?"

Reeve chewed on her bottom lip. "I don't know."

Gage and Patrick joined them on each side.

"You can't be considering this," Patrick hissed.

"I want answers," Aster said, and Reeve agreed.

"But these people could be working with Eben. And witchcraft —what if it's dark magic?" Patrick countered.

Gage was surprisingly silent, and Aster peered up at him to see if his expression gave away his thoughts. He was looking at her, and when their eyes met, he leaned forward, placing a soft kiss on her lips. "I trust you."

She slipped her hand into his and gave it a squeeze.

"Reeve?" Aster turned to her sister. She wasn't doing this without her.

The woman who claimed to be their mom called across the room. "Girls, you don't remember this, but I taught you to always listen to your heart and your gut. Your instincts won't steer you wrong. Listen to them now. What are they telling you?"

Sound advice, something a parent would give. Tuning out everything else, Aster followed that advice and turned her focus inward. That feeling she had earlier was still there; something was telling her that these strangers weren't really strangers.

"Let's do this," Reeve said, having come to the same conclusion. She stepped away from them and approached Harlow. "What happens now?"

Harlow unrolled the paper in her hand, which turned out to be two sheets of paper with a variation of a Celtic knot drawn onto them.

"This is a symbol for family," she explained. "Once I transfer these temporary tattoos to your skin, the memory spell will be triggered. So where do you want them?"

Reeve didn't even hesitate. She was wearing a short-sleeved shirt and held her arm out so the creamy, smooth underside faced up. She pointed at her wrist. Patrick moved to stand beside her, and Aster sensed the tension radiating off of him. His jaw was clenched tight, and his lips were pressed into an austere line. He stood with his knees soft and legs hip width apart, ready to jump into action if anything hinky happened once the tattoo was in place.

Aster watched every detail. Harlow set one of the sheets of paper over Reeve's wrist and placed her palm over the design.

"Restore but only memories that are pure. Family bonds that were lost are now found. For twenty-eight days, these terms shall be bound," she recited. Blue flames licked out from beneath her hand, and the edges of the paper turned black and curled before disintegrating into gray ash that disappeared before it could hit the floor. Harlow removed her hand, revealing the tattoo, the bold, black design a stark contrast against Reeve's pale skin.

Then it was Aster's turn. She held her right arm out, pointing at the same spot on her wrist as Reeve. Harlow repeated the process, and Aster braced for a burn, expecting the blue flames to cause some sort of pain, but they only emitted a soothing warmth that seeped into her skin and traveled through her veins like a dose of morphine. As the warmth moved into her brain, it was like something unlocked. This time, when she looked at the older couple, they weren't strangers.

"Mom? Dad?" Saying that came so naturally, and the knowledge was suddenly there that they were her parents, and she had only ever known them as Mom and Dad.

Her mom launched out of the chair, pulling Aster and her sister into a hug, which their dad immediately joined. Their combined scents along with the familiar comfort of their embrace was too much, and Aster started to cry. She wasn't the only one. They were all sobbing and holding onto each other.

Faint memories arose of sitting on her dad's lap in the cab of an excavator as he let her take the controls. A skinned knee being carefully cleaned with her mom's gentle touch. A field full of wildflowers almost as tall as Aster as she chased after her sister. Lying on her back and staring up at the sun, only to have it blocked out by an older boy as he stood over her laughing. Braden. Where was Braden? She pulled back as the void of her missing brother grew wider, heavier. Something horrible lurked in the recesses of her memories.

"Oh, my girls, we missed you so much!" Her mom sniffled, wiping tears from her cheeks. She smiled and cupped Aster's face and then Reeve's. Her hands were warm and soft.

"I don't understand. You knew where we were. Why did you let us go so long?" Reeve asked.

Their parents exchanged a look, and her dad's smile faded. "That's a long story, and it all starts with Damian Stone."

That name drop was as effective as throwing a live grenade in the room. Everyone was alert and on defense, Gage especially.

"What do you know about Damian?" he demanded.

"I know that he killed our son, and he's the reason why our girls were forced to leave their hometown. And I know you killed him to protect Aster. I'll never be able to thank you enough." Her dad clapped Gage on his shoulder.

"Braden is dead?" Aster gasped at the same time as Reeve. That explained the dread she felt earlier. Her mom pulled them into another hug and fresh tears fell as they mourned for their brother.

Gage stepped behind Aster and placed his hand on her back, using his thumb to rub small, soothing circles. "Damian was following Reeve. I remember tracking him. I remember killing him, but it's always been hazy. I couldn't remember all the details, especially where I killed him. Now it makes sense. The memory spell?"

"Yes. It's one of the most effective ways to protect our town," her dad said.

"Jesus Christ." Gage moved away, and Aster immediately missed his presence at her back. Pulling away from her mom and sister, she followed her mate across the room, where he stood looking out the window. She knew he was seeing beyond their neighborhood to where the woods beckoned. His inner cat was probably urging him to shift, to run and hunt to work out the problems he was facing in his human life. If only it were that easy.

Aster hugged him from behind, wrapping her arms around his waist and burying her face in the center of his broad back. Her mate was an alpha, through and through; a tough but fair leader and a masterful fighter who taught others to fight at his gym. He was kind, intelligent, and strong beyond measure, but the past two years, Mina's disappearance, and now this revelation that Damian had killed his mate's brother and that everything was connected was taking a toll. She felt it through their mate bond. He practically vibrated with frustration and anger. Gage placed a hand over hers and relaxed. She felt his muscles release, and he leaned back into her hug.

"I'm sorry about your brother," he said.

"Me too."

"Are you okay?"

"No," she admitted with a soft laugh. "This is a lot to process and there isn't time." Moving around so she stood in front of Gage, she looked up at him. Stubble grew along his strong jawline where he was normally clean shaven. There were shadows under his blue eyes, evidence of the sleepless nights they had both endured since Mina was taken. His hair was short on the sides, but where it was longer on the top, it stood in disarray from him constantly running his hands through it. She was surprised he hadn't started going bald from the repetitive motion, like when a path is worn in grass from people walking on it. She placed her hands on his arms and squeezed. "We can't fall apart now. We need to find Mina. I'll be damned if I let these purist fuckers take another member of my family away."

"Exactly," Reeve said from behind them. Aster and Gage turned to where she and Patrick stood. "As much as I want to go on the search, I'm still lactating and have to pump every few hours. I'll slow you down."

"You pissed me off suggesting I stay back," Patrick said to Gage. "But I've had time to think about it, and as much as I don't like it, you're right. I'll stay with Reeve, and we'll sniff out if there are any more traitors among us."

"Thanks, man," Gage said, and pulled Patrick into a bro hug. They clapped each other on the back, and when they separated, Aster thought she saw a glimmer of tears, but they'd never admit it.

"Just promise us you'll bring our daughter home." Reeve palmed her stomach, a habit she had developed when she was pregnant. She didn't have a baby bump anymore and in fact, had lost too much weight since Mina was taken. Reeve was usually pale, but always had a glow about her. That too had diminished.

"We promise," Aster said.

It was well past midnight before a plan was in place. Willing to trust relative strangers rather than members of his own den, Gage decided that Ryker, Orion, Harlow, Paisley, and Aster's parents were going to be part of the search party. Orion was a skilled tracker, and Ryker could fight. Paisley had healing abilities in case medical attention was required on their trip, and when Aster asked Harlow what she brought to the table, the witch flashed a mysterious smile and said, "I have skills. Don't you worry."

Before Reeve and Patrick left to go back to their townhouse, Reeve hugged Aster tight. "Please be careful," she pleaded. "I can't lose you too."

"I will. Take care of yourself. Hopefully we'll be back before you even notice we're gone. I love you."

"I love you too." They hugged again before Reeve went to their parents to say goodbye.

The group planned to leave at sunrise, giving them a few hours to sleep. Aster showed her parents to the guest bedroom, while Gage took Harlow and Ryker to the office, where there was a futon. Orion was happy to sleep outside on the back patio and stretched out on the chaise lounge underneath the stars. Paisley curled up on the sofa, and Aster turned off lights as their unexpected guests settled in. Gage had gone upstairs to their bedroom, but she couldn't sleep and only had a few hours to kill before sunrise, so she found herself in the kitchen, pulling out ingredients. She put a pot of coffee on to brew while she made a batch of blueberry scones. That's where Gage found her as the sky was beginning to lighten. His eyes were bloodshot, so she didn't think he had slept much, if at all.

"Woman, you're killing me. I smelled these baking all the way upstairs!" He grabbed a scone and ate half in one bite, groaning as he chewed.

Paisley appeared next, yawning as she stumbled into the kitchen. "I thought I smelled your famous scones! Can I have one?"

"Help yourself. What do you mean, famous?"

"You won Best of Hickory Farms two years in a row. Wait, not Hickory Farms." She shook her head as if trying to shake sense into it. "These are award winning and my own personal addiction." She bit into one and sighed. "You left the recipe with Willow at Coffee Haven, and they're still amazing, but nothing like when you make them."

It was so weird having someone talk about parts of her life that she didn't remember. While she had memories of her parents and family, and there had been some vague recollections of her childhood, Paisley was still a stranger to her. They obviously had a history, though.

Soon, they were joined by everyone else, who all looked the worse for wear except for Orion, who bounced around with nervous energy. Coffee was poured and scones devoured. Aster packed up the rest to take with them on the road and cleaned the kitchen before going upstairs to take a quick shower, knowing it might be her last for a while.

At dawn, the group piled into the van Ryker had acquired and headed out to Buena Vista—the last probable location of Eben and his demented band of followers. All thoughts were on the mission: bring Mina home.

CHAPTER 7

*T*he van was like one a tour company or church group would use for an excursion: generic white exterior with a lot of windows and on the inside, three rows of bench seats with plenty of room in the rear for storage. Ryker was driving with Orion riding shotgun. Gage and Aster sat in the first row, Mike and Anne behind them, with Paisley and Harlow in the last row, both fast asleep. Mike held Anne's hand, and they both seemed content to sit there and watch Aster.

Physically, she hadn't changed much over the past two years. Her wavy red hair was still long, and she had the same athletic figure, but there were subtle differences. She'd always had this intensity about her, like she was ready for the day to be over with so she could move on to the next thing. Whether she grew out of it or Gage softened her edge, Mike didn't know, but he thought it was a good change. She hadn't lost her temper. He and Anne had heard the argument going on between their daughter and her mate while they waited outside their house. She hadn't backed down an inch, and that made Mike smile. He knew where Gage was coming from but learned a long time ago not to pull that kind of shit. He would have been disappointed if Aster had let him get away with it.

Now Aster slept, her head on Gage's shoulder, bobbing slightly with the motion of the van, and Mike knew it was because she'd stayed awake the night before. He had too. He'd lain in bed next to Anne and heard Aster moving around in the kitchen, which was directly below the guest room. He had been tempted to go down and spend time with her but knew her well enough to let her be. She usually baked to clear her head, the same way Reeve had to clean when she was mad.

They had mapped out a loose plan the night before. Once they were in Buena Vista, which was about a two-hour drive from Denver, Gage would call the coven leader about their witch who was missing. While Gage was meeting with the coven, the rest of the group was going to spread out and canvas shops to ask locals if they had seen Eben or Alice. Everyone had taken pictures of the surveillance images with their phones. Hopefully somebody in this town saw something.

The drive was beautiful and scenic. Highway 285 cut through valleys with trees rising on each side, fading away to rocky peaks, some still covered with patches of snow. They passed raging rivers, the rapids fed by melting snow pack, and the forest called to Mike, his inner cat itching to explore. They pulled into Buena Vista, a quaint old mining town with a main street that reminded him of Havenwood Falls. Storefronts lined each side, offering everything from coffee to gear rentals for rafting, fishing, and mountain biking. The town was just waking up, and the coffee shop's outdoor seating area was full. Ryker found parking on the street and expertly maneuvered the large van into the spot. Most of the vehicles parked along the street had either kayaks or canoes strapped to the roofs, or had bike racks on the back, loaded with mountain bikes. One Subaru had a bumper sticker that said *I'm fly and so is my fishing.*

Gage nudged Aster awake, and she sat up, blinking to clear her eyes. Mike watched as she stretched her neck and yawned. She had a sleepy disoriented and dazed look on her face when she glanced over her shoulder at him before climbing out of the van. She stretched again once she was standing on the sidewalk, a languid stretch that was very feline. Harlow and Paisley looked just as disoriented as they took in their new surroundings. Gage stayed inside the van and called the witch. Their conversation didn't last long before Gage climbed out of the van.

"I'm meeting her at a crystal shop in an hour." He looked at his watch. "How about we meet here at eleven o'clock. That should give us time to ask around."

They all split up, and Mike felt anxious watching his wife and daughter walk away. They weren't going far, but he had just gotten Aster back, and it was hard enough saying goodbye to Reeve, whom they had even less time with.

Since it was still early, not a lot of retail stores were open yet. Mike discovered the hardware store was open. It had a display out front of hanging plants with pink and purple blossoms. They swayed in the light breeze. Gardening tools and other summer essentials were on a rack by the front door, marked as perfect gifts for dad. This made Mike pause. He had forgotten that Sunday was Father's Day. It was a day he tried to forget, since that was the day Aster and Reeve left Havenwood Falls, just after he buried his son. Now he had his daughters back. Thinking of Reeve reminded him that Patrick was being robbed of celebrating his first Father's Day. This just added to his determination to find Mina. He opened the front door to the store, and a little bell chimed. He looked up to see a small brass bell attached to a hook, similar to the one at Coffee Haven. The shop had a resident dog that picked his head up from where it was lying on a dog bed soaked in a pool of sunshine. The dog sniffed the air and growled, baring its teeth at Mike. He almost started laughing, because the Chihuahua was not even a little bit intimidating. The poor thing would probably piss all over himself if he encountered Mike in his mountain lion form. He ignored the dog and approached the customer service desk at the center of the store. An older man was working the register, busy putting price tags on bottles of lighter fluid.

"Good morning, sir," Mike said cheerily, and leaned against the counter. "It sure is a beautiful one, isn't it?"

"Sure is, and it's about time. We had a cold, damp spring. What can I do for you?" The old man pushed his glasses up on his nose and peered at Mike.

"I have an odd request. My friend has a cousin who went off his antidepressants. He's not in his right mind and has gone missing. The police won't file a missing person report because he's an adult. Anyway, I'm helping my friend get the word out, and I'm wondering if you've seen this man—maybe he bought something here in the past week?" Mike held his phone up with the picture of Eben on display. The man squinted his eyes and pulled the phone closer with a liver-spotted hand before shaking his head. "How about this woman? He was last seen getting in a car with her. He was probably hitchhiking." Mike swiped to the picture of Alice and held his phone up again. This time recognition flickered in the old man's eyes.

"Yes. She was in here earlier this week. A fine-looking woman. I won't be forgetting that face anytime soon."

"Monday or Tuesday? Can you be more specific? And was she with anyone else?"

"Nope, she was alone. Let me think." The old man stared off into space for a few seconds before smacking the counter. "That's right. She was here Tuesday. I remember because that was the last day of our buy-one-get-one-free sale on solar-powered lanterns, and she bought the last four we had in stock."

"Thank you! Every little bit of information helps." Mike bought a bottle of water for the man's trouble and left. The Chihuahua raised his hackles at Mike when he walked by.

He texted the information to Gage and moved on to the next business. By the time eleven o'clock rolled around, he had visited ten businesses and received more tips. Eben and Alice were both busy on Monday buying camping supplies, increasing the odds they were preparing to disappear into the woods. This was the consensus with the group as they all exchanged their results. One

49

of Alice's purchases had been diapers—evidence that Mina was still with them.

"So we're heading into the woods?" Aster asked.

"Yes. Eben's Suburban was found just outside of town on a back road near a youth camp. We'll go there and see if we can pick up a scent trail," Gage answered.

"I agree with Gage," Ryker said. "When I was younger and on the run, I went off the grid and hid in the mountains. We passed a Tractor Supply on the way in. We should stop and get camping supplies now. This way we don't lose time circling back."

"Agreed," Mike said. "Someday you'll have to tell me that story."

An hour later, the van was loaded up with camping supplies. They purchased the minimum since they'd have to carry it with them, and if all of the shifters shifted at one point, that would leave Harlow and Paisley with the burden. After a quick lunch in town, they arrived at the site where Eben had torched his vehicle. The Suburban was gone, but scorch marks remained on the ground, and there were discolorations where fluids had seeped into the dirt.

Gage had a sweater that belonged to the witch who had gone missing. He passed it around to the shifters in the group, so they could commit her scent to memory. They had already sniffed a blanket of Mina's and a hat that Alice left behind at the apartment she abandoned. As if on cue, all of the shifters lifted their noses in the air and started to sniff. Orion went one step further and stripped out of his clothes, shifting into his lion form seconds later. He was a sight to behold in the Colorado wilderness. His golden mane rippled in the light breeze, and his tail swished back and forth as he padded across the scorched earth. He chuffed once and pointed his nose toward the south.

"Unbelievable. He picked up a scent already?" Paisley's mouth hung open in shock.

"Told ya he's one of the best trackers," Ryker said with pride. He pulled out his phone and sent a text before opening the back of the van and unloading their supplies. "Load up. We'll follow Orion."

"What about the van? We can't just leave it here, can we?"

Ryker handed a backpack to Paisley. "I texted the coordinates to one of my brothers in the Denver chapter of SIN. It's their van, and they'll send a crew to retrieve it."

"Just like that?" Paisley's eyebrows lifted, and her violet eyes grew wide.

"Yup."

And just like that, they started hiking. Orion had shifted back to his human form and was in the lead, following the scent of the missing witch. They were still too close to civilization for him to be roaming the forest. An African lion sighting would garner attention, and they needed to keep a low profile. The men naturally flanked the women, Ryker picking up the rear while Mike and Gage each took a side.

They kept a steady pace, walking parallel with a creek and stopping occasionally to drink water. When their bottles became empty, they filled them up at the nearest source, and Harlow worked her magic, using a spell that purified the water. Breaks didn't last long, and there wasn't a lot of talking. Mike was focused on his surroundings. He didn't want to miss any sign or clue that would lead them to Mina.

As the shadows grew long and the sun began to dip below the tree line, they started looking for a place to camp for the night. Luck was on their side when they stumbled across an abandoned campsite with a fire pit ready to go: a circle of charred river rocks full of ashes with large logs for seating. Mike and Anne set up the tent while Harlow and Ryker went searching for firewood. Gage and Orion checked the perimeter while Aster and Paisley pulled out food for dinner. Collapsible bowls were set out with plastic spoons. The single pot they bought in Buena Vista was filled with water and dehydrated stew mix. As soon as Ryker and Harlow returned, logs were placed in the fire pit, and with a snap of her fingers, Harlow produced a flame and ignited the kindling. Aster set the pot in the flames, and it didn't take long for the soup to come to a boil. She reached in to grab the handle and hissed, pulling back, cradling her hand against her chest.

"Honey, let me see." Anne was by Aster's side in a second to inspect the damage. From where Mike was sitting across the way, he could see the ugly red mark, a blister already forming.

"I got this, Mrs. M.," Paisley announced, and sat down on Aster's other side. Anne released Aster's hand and watched as Paisley wrapped her fingers around Aster's wrist, then closed her eyes. Mike wasn't sure what was going on, and he thought maybe Paisley fell asleep or was in a trance, she remained so still except for the occasional flicker of movement beneath her eyelids. Aster's gasp drew his attention to her hand. The blister had burst, and the stretched skin sloughed off as the redness began to fade. Within seconds, Aster's hand was completely healed, and Paisley opened her eyes to inspect her work.

"That's amazing," Anne said in awe.

"What's going on? Babe, are you okay?" Gage dropped a dead rabbit on the ground and kneeled in front of his mate.

"I'm fine. I burned my hand, and Paisley healed me. She's a freaking miracle worker. You can't even tell." She flexed her hand and held it up to the firelight. Gage reached for her hand and kissed her palm, then thanked Paisley.

"It's what I do. I'm pre-med right now, but I don't think I want to study human medicine. I'm interested in supernatural healing. In fact, I'll be trying out next month for a new college. It's only for supernaturals. Supposedly there's a healing arts program. I hope I get accepted."

"Yes, Roxy is going through the trials, too," Mike added.

"Well, consider me your patient," Aster said to Paisley with a smile.

Then Paisley noticed the dead rabbit by her feet, and she squealed, lifting her feet off the ground. "I made soup. I am not cooking that! The poor bunny still has fur on it!"

Harlow whipped her head around in horror.

"Who did this?" she demanded, pointing at the body, tears starting to well in her eyes. Ryker rushed over, pulling her into his arms and turning her away from the dead rabbit.

"Her familiar is a snowshoe hare," he explained.

"Sorry, I didn't know," Gage apologized, picking up his kill.

"Paisley, I'll take care of this." Aster took the rabbit from Gage and grabbed a knife from one of the backpacks. She started walking toward the stream nearby, and Mike jogged after her to help.

"You know, I taught you how to clean rabbits and fish when you were little." He fell into step beside her, and she looked up at him with a grin.

Rocks crowded the riverbanks, and Aster chose a large, flat one to clean and skin the rabbit on. She tossed the skin and entrails in the water, the heavy current whisking them away. After rinsing the knife and her bloody hands in the water, she dried her hands on her jeans then sat back on the ground and looked at him. "Can I ask you a question?"

"Anything, baby girl." He sat on a nearby rock and stretched his legs out.

"This memory spell is for twenty-eight days only, right?"

He nodded and picked a pebble up off the ground and tossed it in the water.

"What happens after those days are up?"

Mike hesitated, and her eyes narrowed at him.

"What aren't you telling me?"

With a sigh, he leaned forward and wrapped his arms around his knees. "You can come back home, and as long as you visit once every twenty-eight days, you'll keep your memories. Your banishment was for two years only."

"Okay. Reeve, too?" He hesitated again, and Aster frowned. "Hers is longer, isn't it?"

"Yes, a lot longer. Reeve was permanently banished."

"What?" Aster was on her feet in a blur of motion, her red ponytail flying like a whip in the air when she rounded on him.

"What the hell? That's beyond unfair. That's downright cruel! You mean to tell me she can never go back?"

Mike hung his head, his heart breaking all over again. "Yes, and your mother and I won't be able to contact her."

This brought her up short. "Which is why you never visited us." She sat down on the rock next to him. "What horrid rules. Why didn't you leave?"

"We talked about it, but we have a lot invested in the town. Your nephew needs us, and the den needs us, too. Your mother and I knew you two would be okay. You're both adults, and we know we raised you right. Plus, you found your mates and had your own lives to live."

"So all of us got a pretty shitty deal, huh?" She rose to her feet and picked up the rabbit, walking away without waiting for him to answer. Mike followed, quickly catching up to her. Her head was down, and she was silent as they walked side by side.

"Penny for your thoughts?" It was something he always said to her when she was younger and lost in her head.

She gave him a sad smile. "Just thinking about whether I want to go back to Havenwood Falls at all."

He stopped walking, because that statement might as well have been delivered with a roundhouse kick to his stomach. Would the fates be so cruel as to make him lose his youngest daughter a second time?

That night there was a deep divide between him and Aster. She erected a wall and huddled close to her mate as they sat around the fire eating. Gage roasted the rabbit and divided it equally among the shifters. Paisley and Harlow were too grossed out and made their displeasure known while they stuck with soup. Anne kept giving him questioning looks, which meant she noticed the distance.

The distance continued until the fourth day, which is when the faint scent trail for the witch grew stronger. They were deep in the forest now. In the beginning, they crossed paths with numerous people, and at night, smoke from nearby campfires filled the air, but each day they hiked farther into the wild, there were fewer and fewer people. Orion paused in front of a pinyon pine and plucked three brown hairs off a cluster of needles.

"Jackpot!"

Gage sniffed the hairs and scowled. His eyes scanned the trees that surrounded them.

"What's wrong?" Aster asked.

"It's always the witch's scent. We haven't picked up even the slightest trace of Mina or Alice. What if this trail is intentionally leading us astray?"

"Or it's leading us to them. Remember, this witch was allegedly taken against her will," Harlow responded. "She could be leaving us breadcrumbs."

"This is taking too long!" Gage growled, and ran a hand through his hair. His eyes flashed a golden amber. That night was the full moon, and they were all feeling its pull. The urge to shift and roam the forest was driving Mike to the edge.

"Listen," he said. "Let's keep following the trail and tonight, we'll shift and follow our instincts. I think we're all going a little crazy, am I right?"

"Fuck yes!" Orion cheered, and tore off his shirt. "I'm ready now."

"Simmer down, shifter. Mr. M. said tonight," Paisley said.

"You like this, Goldie?" Orion ran his hands over his bare chest, and Paisley rolled her eyes, which only encouraged Orion, who kept his shirt off, stuffing it in a pocket of the backpack Anne was carrying. Mike couldn't help but laugh at the antics. Oh, to be young again.

That night, once the campsite was set up and the group had eaten dinner, the shifters left their clothes, plus Harlow and Paisley, behind. They slipped between the trees, the moon bathing everything in silver light, and shifted. They ran as a group, yipping with joy at the freedom of giving over to their animal halves. Aster and Anne were similar in coloring and had reddish-brown-tipped ears. Anne had a white spot on her forehead and was a little bigger than her daughter. For the first hour they ran and hunted just to get it out of their system. Ryker chuffed and started sniffing the ground, looking more like a bloodhound than a lion. His dark brown mane dragged in the dirt, picking up leaves and pine needles. Mike inhaled deeply and noticed the witch's scent was strong. Right beneath that, not as strong, he detected his granddaughter's scent. Then he was off following the trail. He heard the thud of paws behind him and turned back to see Aster and Anne coming up on his rear. They raced up a steep incline that evened out to a plateau that turned out to be an abandoned campsite. Here the smells were concentrated, but they weren't fresh. He searched the area, leading with his nose, and found a baby's sock half buried in the loose soil underneath a shrub. Mina's scent saturated the fabric. His instinct told him they were on the right trail, and they were getting closer.

CHAPTER 8

*A*ster was tired and dirty. She dreamed of showers and indoor plumbing. If she had to sleep one more night in the tent when Orion had gas, she was going to lose it. They had been following the scent trail and knew they were getting closer, but they had been in pursuit for over two weeks. A solar-powered charger for her cell phone had been a much-needed connection to Reeve who, the last time they spoke, sounded despondent. Time was running out on the memory spell, too. She didn't have many memories to lose. It was like she had an internal countdown clock, and as each day passed, the sense of urgency grew. Aster hoped their luck was about to change. The trail they had been following was the freshest one yet, and along the river bank, where they stopped to refill water containers, new paw prints were pressed into the mud, made by more than one mountain lion.

The group approached a clearing, and Aster caught glimpses of tents through the trees. As they drew closer, she could see the tents were set up in a circle around a fire pit and in front of a small cabin. Wood smoke and voices carried on the light breeze that rustled leaves, disguising their approach. The breeze also blew their scents away from the camp. A strong whiff of her niece's scent caused Aster's nostrils to flare.

Orion, who was leading the group, stopped. His ears moved back and forth, and his mane rippled in the wind. He had been tracking in his lion form since they were so deep in the forest, the chances of running across a human slim. Being in his lion form heightened his senses, and he could provide the first line of defense if their presence was discovered.

In fact, all of the men had shifted into their animal forms as a defensive measure, and that was why Ryker was in the back of the pack. Gage and Aster's dad flanked each side, protecting the women. The sexist strategy had pissed Aster off, but she couldn't refute it was a sound strategy. The stronger members provided a well-fortified barrier. She still didn't like it and was tempted to run past Orion. Her niece was close, and if she was right, Mina was being held in the cabin.

Aster stopped, tensed, and poised to shift at the slightest indication the group's approach had been discovered. Minutes passed by, and a drop of sweat rolled down her spine, tickling, but she didn't dare move. The forest around them remained still and undisturbed. She slowly let out her breath and loosened her stance, unclenching her hands, which had automatically balled into fists. Gage had told her that would happen. She had been training with him at the Sweat Box after she expressed her desire to learn to fight and defend herself while in her human form. When she had complained about the repetitiveness of her training sessions, Gage told her she was training her body to respond on muscle memory. "When fight or flight mode kicks in, your muscles will know to fight. That's the goal, babe. You won't even have to think. Just act. It will help to control your shift, too. Less chance of public exposure."

Looking down at the half-moon impressions in the palms of her hands from her fingernails, Aster grinned. All the hard work had been worth it.

Orion took a step forward, the sound of his giant paws absorbed by the spongy moss blanketing the forest floor. His movement caught Aster's attention, and she dropped her hands to her sides. In unison, the group moved with Orion until only two stands of trees separated them from the camp, which looked like some modern gypsy encampment. Ropes were tied to tree trunks to form clotheslines, where an older woman with salt and pepper hair coiled in a bun was hanging up a shirt to dry. She was talking to a younger woman who was heavy with child. Her sundress couldn't disguise her round belly. A folding chair outside a brown tent had an acoustic guitar propped against it. Not a lot of sunlight filtered through the canopy that loomed overhead, so it seemed later than early afternoon. A shirtless man crouched in front of the fire pit, placing fresh wood in the middle of a circle of blackened stones. Large logs encircled the pit for seating. There was something vaguely familiar about his movements. His back was to them, and a long scar that started at his neck and stopped just before the waist of his jeans jogged her memory. Aster suspected, if he turned around, there'd be an even bigger scar on his chest and abdomen. Gage had caused those wounds when he went toe to toe—or paw to paw—with the guy. They had finally found Eben Brant.

Two years earlier, Eben had challenged Gage for leadership after Gage had killed Damian. After Gage won, he had ordered Eben to be exiled immediately. Eben limped away, holding his skin together and leaving a trail of blood. That was the last they had seen or heard of him.

Aster glanced over at Gage and saw he was crouched low, ears flat, nostrils flaring. A low growl rattled deep in his throat. His gaze was fixed on Eben. She reached over and placed a hand on his back, and the growling subsided. The last thing they needed was to give up their location. They were lucky to have made it that far undetected.

Suddenly, a shrill cry pierced the stillness—a cry Aster recognized—and it came from the cabin. She wanted to sprint across the clearing and barge in, but that would be reckless. There were others around, and she didn't know who was in the cabin with her niece.

Harlow whispered, and a shimmering wave radiated out from her palm, settling over everyone before the group fanned out, threading their way through the trees to circle the clearing. The spell Harlow had cast was basically a stealth spell that muted any noise.

"I want to check the back of the cabin to see if there's another door. Going in through the back will add an element of surprise," Aster said to Harlow as they moved closer to the structure. Their movements were slow. Using trees trunks for cover, they inched forward. A shout echoed across the clearing, and chaos erupted as men shifted into mountain lions, leaving piles of tattered clothes on the ground. Aster held her breath as Gage and Eben went head to head. It was déjà vu.

"Come on," Harlow urged, gripping Aster's elbow. "Our guys will be fine. Let's take advantage of the diversion."

They sprinted to the back of the cabin and discovered a screen door. Aster wrenched it open and charged inside, Harlow right on her heels. The cabin was small and extremely rustic, a basic structure. There wasn't any plumbing, and the single room was cluttered with stained mattresses on the floor. A woman was lying on one of the mattresses. Her hair was unkempt and greasy, her white nightgown tinged a dingy gray. Aster's eyes adjusted to the dim lighting, and she noticed the woman was restrained. Rope ties around her wrists and ankles were tethered to what looked like handles, nailed to the rough floorboards, similar to how a boat was tied to a dock. The woman looked at Aster with dull eyes as if she was resigned to her fate. Remembering Reeve's story about how she was held captive in what was basically a breeding house made Aster's rage rise to the surface. She completed scanning the room and zeroed in on the older woman cowering in the corner, curled protectively over a baby. A tuft of strawberry blond hair stood up beyond the crook of the woman's arm. Relief at seeing her niece alive and in the same room flooded Aster, and she blinked tears away. She couldn't relax until she had Mina in her arms. The sound of the fighting outside grew louder. Aster saw Ryker and

Orion attacking four mountain lions. They had their backs to each other and were swatting the smaller cats away like they were swatting at flies.

"Alice, give me Mina so we can end this without any more bloodshed," Aster said to the woman. She approached with her hands open and palms up, as a sign of peace even though she wanted to freak out on the woman who had baked the laced brownies and pretended to be nice, just to get close to Mina.

The older woman growled and spit in the direction of Aster's feet. Her dark eyes shone with malice, and she clutched Mina closer to her chest.

"Come any closer and the babe is dead." She moved so Aster could see that Alice's hands had shifted into paws. Long, sharp claws threatened to puncture her niece's skin.

"You wouldn't," Aster challenged. "She's a pureblood. That's why you stole her, isn't it?" Aster wasn't going to reveal that Mina's blood wasn't pure. Yes, she was the granddaughter of an alpha, but her great-grandmother was human. Revealing that information would make Mina less valuable. When Damian had Reeve on his radar, he only zeroed in on her alpha lineage. Aster looked over at Harlow, and her friend dipped her head ever so slightly. She was ready whenever Aster made her move.

"You don't deserve her. We're preserving our species, keeping the blood pure. You're a traitor to our kind if you don't agree."

"You're condoning rape and forced breeding. You're a traitor to your own gender!" The angrier Aster became, the stronger the urge to shift grew. She took a deep breath and exhaled sharply, like a bull getting ready to charge. She was done trying to talk to this woman. It was time to take action.

"Now!" she said, and a second later, Harlow began whispering while flicking the fingers of her other hand. Suddenly, Alice froze. She stared unblinking at them, mouth partly open. Aster quickly walked over and pried her niece free of the psycho's clutches. Part of the blanket she was swaddled in snagged on a claw and ripped, but her niece was unharmed.

"Oh, baby girl!" Aster cried, and hugged her niece tight, breathing in her scent. Mina fussed briefly before yawning and letting out a contented sigh. She snuggled against Aster's chest, and her eyelids drifted closed.

"Look at you with the magic touch," Harlow said, and smiled down at Mina before gently caressing her rosy cheek. "Come on, it sounds like the fight is winding down. We have what we came for, and we should go."

"What about her?" Aster nodded in the direction of the captive woman.

Harlow walked over and knelt down by one side of the mattress and untied the knot, freeing one arm and leg. She then did the other side. Once the woman was free, Harlow gathered up the rope and crossed the room to where Alice stood, still frozen. Harlow manipulated Alice's arms so her hands were behind her back and then tied them together before securing her to an exposed wooden post that ran from floor to ceiling.

"There. That should buy us some time." Harlow spun around, her long, dark hair moving with her, and crossed back to the captive woman. "I've been training with my grandmother," she explained as she knelt down. "I froze you in place once," she said to Aster. "You don't remember, but I can freeze people or objects in place, and I can even stop time. I have more control now, and I've learned how to be selective with what I freeze. It's pretty cool, and it definitely came in handy today."

Harlow placed her hand on the woman's forehead and whispered some words under her breath. Suddenly the woman blinked and shot backwards, away from Harlow's touch.

"What just happened?" she asked, and then hissed when she lifted her arms, stopping to stare with wonder at not being anchored to the floor anymore.

"You're free," Aster said. "You can either come with us or go on your own." She turned and started moving toward the back door. She recognized Harlow's footsteps behind her and then heard a scrambling of someone hurrying after them. She glanced over her shoulder, holding her niece protectively against her chest, and saw the woman they just freed move behind Harlow. Aster tensed and opened her mouth to shout out a warning to her friend.

"Wait—please!" The woman held her hands up and took a step back. "I'm not a threat. I have no idea where I am and want to come with you. Can you help me?"

Aster looked the woman up and down. She wore cheap dollar-store flip-flops and the ragged nightgown. Aster sniffed the air to gauge the woman's scent. She didn't smell any aggression, just fear. Her posture was akin to her showing her belly and submitting. Aster didn't sense any deception either, so she agreed.

"Stick close to us and be quiet," she said, and opened the back door, preparing to fight only to discover her mom and Paisley waiting outside in the shade. Aster's mom's eyes went right to the baby in her arms, and she rushed forward.

"Is this Mina?" she asked, her voice cracking. Tears welled as she gazed upon her granddaughter for the first time.

"Do you want to hold her?" Aster shifted Mina, making sure to cradle her head, and handed her over.

"Hi, little one," Anne whispered to the sleeping baby. "I'm your grandmother. Or grandma. Maybe you'll call me Nana or Yaya. We'll see what you wind up calling me."

Aster smiled at the sight. Despite her limited memories, she was beginning to view Mike and Anne less as strangers that showed up on her doorstep and more as parents. Whatever bond was severed two years earlier was slowly knitting itself back together.

"She looks just like your sister at this age. A spitting image," Anne said. "You were both such beautiful babies."

"Aster, you didn't tell me your mom was such a badass fighter," Paisley said. "You should have seen her. We stayed behind in the woods, out of sight of the clearing, but a mountain lion snuck up on us from the opposite direction of the camp, and holy fairies! The next thing I see is your mom shifting, basically in midair. Her paws had barely hit the ground before she was charging the guy.

She had him pinned, and I'm pretty sure castrated, or is it neutered?" She looked at Anne for confirmation.

"Either one works," she said with a shrug.

"It was epic! I need to learn to fight like that. Wow!"

"Are you guys okay?" Aster asked, looking for any signs of injury.

"We're fine, honey, and so is everyone else. I think the men are just toying with their prey now."

Harlow sighed and rolled her eyes.

"Cats are gonna cat, aren't they?" she asked, which caused Aster and her mom to burst out laughing.

They walked around the cabin, and Aster peered around the corner to make sure it was safe to move forward. Her mom was right—the guys had everything under control, but based on the carnage lying on the ground, they had surrendered to their animal instincts at one point. All of the purists were dead or in the process of bleeding out into the dirt, with the exception of the pregnant woman Aster had seen earlier. She was being restrained by a naked Orion, who had shifted back into his human form. Gage had also shifted back but had put on a pair of jeans. That's when Aster realized Paisley and her mom had the backpacks with their belongings. They hadn't left them behind in the trees.

"Orion didn't want pants?" Aster asked Paisley, and watched with amusement as she blushed so hard even her ears turned pink.

"I tried, but he told me he wants me to see what I've been turning down." Paisley pretended to gag, and Aster grinned when she caught the young fae checking Orion out. He was pretty spectacular to look at, she had to admit, and well equipped in all areas.

"Don't knock it till you try it, P," Harlow said. "You know what they say—once you go cat, you never go back. That's a true story." She winked, and Paisley's fair skin turned an even deeper shade of pink.

"Oh, absolutely. The things they can do with their tongues," Aster teased, and Harlow laughed as Paisley flipped them both off.

"Girls, really?" Anne admonished, which only made Harlow and Aster laugh harder. Once she started laughing, she couldn't stop. All of the stress and adrenaline from the past two weeks was over. Aster imagined she seemed a little manic, since she was losing her shit while mutilated bodies were scattered about, but that didn't matter. It felt good to release.

"What's so funny, Country Club?" Ryker asked as he sauntered toward them. He had shifted back to his human form and was completely naked, his scarred, tattooed, and extremely muscular body on full display. Aster knew not to gawk and averted her eyes. Shifters were used to nudity—it was part of the life. She had been naked countless of times in front of the den. Ryker's appearance did get her to stop laughing.

"Oh, for fuck's sake, Crusher. Put some pants on!" Harlow unzipped the bag Paisley was carrying and pulled out a pair of jeans and tossed them to her mate.

"Jealous, babe?"

"No. I know you're mine. I just don't want the whole world seeing your junk. Especially Mrs. McCabe."

A low, rumbly chuckle resonated from Ryker as he pulled on the jeans.

"Who's she?" Ryker asked, nodding in the direction of the woman they had freed. She stood off to the side, her arms wrapped tightly around her body as she surveyed the massacre. Out in the daylight, her appearance was even worse. There were burns on her skin from where the rope had been tied around her ankles and wrists. Bruises, varying in shades from black to yellow, marred her arms. The discoloration stood out against her pale skin.

"She was tied up in the cabin, and she wants to come with us," Aster explained.

"Tied up?" Ryker shook his head. "Those fucking sick bastards. Hey, girl, you got a name?" he called out to the woman, who jumped at his booming voice.

"I'll go talk to her." Aster approached the woman, who seemed

65

to shrink into herself. "I'm Aster McCabe," she introduced herself, holding her right hand out.

"Lauren Ericson." After a moment's hesitation, she slipped her trembling hand into Aster's and shook it. "What happened here?" Lauren stared past Aster's shoulder at the carnage.

"These are former members of our den whom we exiled. They kidnapped my niece. My mate is the alpha. We fought, and they lost."

"Good," Lauren said with a sneer. "They kidnapped me, too. Six months ago, I think? They said my blood was pure and precious, and it was my duty to procreate purebloods."

At this admission, Lauren broke down, and Aster felt her own tears threaten to spill. This poor woman had endured the stuff of nightmares. Tentatively, she curled an arm around Lauren's shoulder and let the woman cry.

Aster made eye contact with Paisley and signaled for the young fae to come over. "Paisley, this is Lauren. Can you give her some of my clothes and take her to the stream we passed so she can clean up? Lauren, Paisley is a healer, and if you want, she can check you over and take care of your injuries."

Lauren nodded and wiped her nose with the back of her hand. "That would be nice, thank you."

As Paisley and Lauren walked off together, Aster watched them leave, her heart heavy with the knowledge that Paisley couldn't heal all of Lauren's wounds. It would take years to recover from the emotional damage, if she ever did. Their own kind did this; that's what bothered Aster the most. This group's twisted ideology allowed for them to mistreat their own. It was madness. The past two years had been spent rooting this evil out of their den. Though they were suspicious of everyone, Aster and Reeve had thought they could trust Alice, who was a sweet, grandmotherly type, always doting on Mina. Now they knew it was to serve dark intentions. Where was the loyalty?

A hoarse cry broke through Aster's thoughts, and she turned toward the sound to see her mom trying to soothe Mina.

"I think she's hungry," she told her mom.

"There's formula in Paisley's backpack."

The fire was still going, and there was a pot of water near the edge. It didn't take long to bring the water to a boil and warm up the formula. Once she tested it on the inside of her wrist, Aster brought the bottle to her mom who was sitting on a chair by one of the tents. Her dad was crouched next to her, gently playing with Mina's hair with a look of wonder on his weathered face. Mina greedily accepted the bottle and started sucking on the nipple, her feet kicking happily as she ate.

"Oh crap! I need to let Reeve and Patrick know we found Mina." Aster reached for her cell phone that was in the back pocket of her jeans. She didn't have a signal but tried calling anyway. "Do you have signal?" she asked her parents.

"Check. Our phones are in the bag." Aster found the phones, but they didn't have any reception either.

"Does anyone's phone have a signal?" Aster called out. The moment she asked, the woman Orion had restrained, and whom Gage was questioning, started cackling.

"Wait." Harlow closed her eyes for a few seconds. "It's a spell. We know you're working with a witch. Where is she?"

The woman threw her head back, almost headbutting Orion, and started cackling again. *She is batshit,* Aster thought.

"You know what? I have my own bag of tricks," Harlow said. She walked across the clearing, past the fire pit, to stand in front of the woman, who suddenly stopped laughing and regarded Harlow warily. "See lady, I'm a witch. A powerful witch. I can make you tell me everything we want to know."

Harlow pressed her forefinger against the woman's forehead and whispered a few words. "There. Gage, ask anything. The truth spell prevents her from lying and forces her to answer any questions she is asked."

The woman's eyes grew wide, and she started thrashing, but Orion held firm.

Gage smiled at Harlow before turning his attention to the

woman. With his arms crossed over his bare chest, he was an intimidating sight. "Was this group working with anyone else?"

Clamping her mouth shut, the woman stared stonily at Gage. Aster began to wonder if she was resistant to Harlow's spell, but a few seconds later the woman let out a gasp, like she had been holding her breath, and answered. "No. Eben paid a witch and brought her here to place the spell around the camp. It was supposed to keep technology from working, so if drones flew overhead, we'd be undetectable. We were also supposed to be shielded in a bubble of sorts that kept this camp invisible."

Harlow snorted. "Well, you didn't get your money's worth. Where is the witch?"

"Eben killed her. He was smart and didn't want to leave any trails to lead back to us."

"Were you going to stay here? You wouldn't last through winter." Gage looked around at the camp. "Why go through all the trouble?"

"Eben decided to stop here until I had the baby. Traveling so late in my pregnancy wasn't getting any easier."

"Were you with this group willingly?"

"Yes! Eben was my alpha and my mate. It's an honor to be part of creating a superior line of our species. I know who you are, Gage Barrows. My alpha told me all about you and how you're a traitor to our kind. Your niece was in better hands with us. She would have been raised the right way. The pure way."

Aster felt sick listening to this woman spew her rhetoric. She approached Gage and hooked her hand in the crook of his arm.

"Are there more of you?" she asked.

The woman faltered, and her eyes shone with tears. "No," she answered with a hoarse whisper. "Not in Colorado, at least. You succeeded in wiping us out." She went limp and started sobbing. "You ruined us!"

Aster's dad joined them, and said, "There are other purist groups throughout the country. It's a growing movement, unfortunately, but it's not new. Your grandfather experienced this ideology back in his day. At least the threat in Colorado has been eliminated . . . for now." He then exchanged a significant look with Gage.

"Something we'll have to keep an eye on," Gage replied.

"Agreed."

Seeing her dad and her mate as equals, alphas working together, made Aster swell with pride and gave her a glimpse of a future with her parents in their lives. It was moments like that when Aster wanted to return to Havenwood Falls, but then she remembered Reeve couldn't be a part of that, and the anger returned, settling in her stomach like a stone.

Just then, Harlow approached and sat down heavily on the ground, leaning back against a tree. "I removed the shielding spell. It was more complex than I thought, but it's done."

Aster grabbed her cell phone and did a happy dance when she saw she had service. She immediately called Reeve, who answered after the first ring.

"Aster, thank god! I was getting so worried! Everybody's phone was going right to voicemail. No one was responding to my texts and then you just dropped off the geo-locating app. Are you okay? Did you find Mina?"

"Yes. We have her, and she's safe. Mom is feeding her as we speak."

"Oh, thank god! Is she okay? Did those bastards hurt her?" Reeve wavered between sobs and fierce momma bear.

"She's fine, Reeve. It looks like they took care of her. Mina didn't have a scratch on her, and her clothes are clean. She hadn't been left to wallow in a dirty diaper, and her cheeks are just as full as before, so she was well fed. I'll send you a picture as soon as we hang up, okay? We have some cleaning up to do here, then we're heading home." She didn't tell her sister that cleanup meant cleaning up a crime scene. Were they going to bury the bodies, burn them, or leave them out in the open for some unsuspecting hiker to stumble across?

She ended the call, hanging up on Reeve, who was still crying tears of relief. Aster couldn't imagine what her sister was going through. Her mom held Mina up for a series of pictures, and Aster sent them to Reeve, who responded with every heart emoji.

The once-combative woman was now docile. Apparently being compelled to tell the truth took a lot out of her. Orion released her arms, and she sank down to the ground, where she stared blankly at the dying embers of the fire.

"What are we going to do with her?" Aster asked Gage.

"We'll have to take her with us. We'll bring her back to Denver and decide what to do with her there," Gage answered.

"What about Alice? Are we bringing her back too?" Aster asked, and Gage turned to look at her.

"Alice?"

"Oh, you don't know, that's right. Alice is tied up in the cabin. She was holding Mina and threatened to kill her."

Gage's nostrils flared with this new information, and he growled, a low rumble that vibrated deep in his chest. "These are unforgivable offenses. She was disloyal, and her acts were a direct attack on den leadership."

"She's a heartless bitch. Add that to her list of offenses." Aster jumped at the voice coming from behind her. Looking over her shoulder, she relaxed when she saw it was Lauren. Paisley had healed the bruises, and the burns on her ankles and wrists were gone.

"And who are you?" Gage ran a hand through his short blond hair before crossing his arms over his chest again, his gaze narrowing on Lauren.

Aster quickly explained how she and Harlow rescued the woman.

"Did Alice mistreat you?" Gage asked.

Lauren nodded, and a visible shudder ran through her before she told them about the tortures she endured during her captivity.

When Gage asked Lauren if she wanted to be the one to kill Alice, she didn't even hesitate. She left them and entered the cabin. Moments later, a scream echoed out into the forest, the trees absorbing the sound. Then there was silence. A squeak of hinges later, Lauren emerged, wiping her hands with a white towel, staining it red with blood.

"It's done," she said, when she joined everyone where they had gathered around the fire pit. She tossed the towel on the dying fire, where it began to smoke.

Death hung in the air around them like the campground now had an aura. A shiver ran down Aster's spine as she surveyed the bodies scattered across the ground. It looked like Jason from the *Friday the 13th* movies had stopped by for a murderous rampage.

"How do you propose we clean this mess up?" she asked Gage. "We can't just leave it like this."

"Burn it," her dad suggested. "Burn it all."

"And start a wildfire? That's too dangerous. These trees will go up like kindling."

"Not necessarily," Harlow said, getting to her feet from where she had been resting against a tree. "You have a witch at your disposal, remember?" She wiggled her fingers, and embers from the fire swirled upwards like a mini tornado.

"Harlow, are you sure? It's a lot to ask you to cover up a crime scene," Aster said. She was in awe that the witch even offered. Aster's memories of Harlow were still vague. She knew they were friends, and that warm, fuzzy feeling she connected with loved ones was there, but she didn't have anything specific to draw on, so the trust was still a little thin.

If she went back to Havenwood Falls, all of her memories would return, or so she was promised. While those memories offered the chance at renewed friendship, she also knew heartache and grief waited for her. Flashes of her brother, Braden, had been surfacing more frequently. She would get glimpses, like looking at a flash of an image before it moved on to the next slide, a flash of Braden, lifeless on the ground, his body broken and bloody.

"I'm sure. It won't be the first crime scene I've covered up."

"What?" She stared at Harlow with her mouth parted, temporarily shocked speechless.

"Oh girl, we have a lot of catching up to do. I'll bring the wine. But first, let's get everyone out of the forest. It's creepy as fuck here." Harlow started to make a portal. Her arm was raised in the air, and a dark sphere began to form right before she dropped her arm and turned toward Orion. Placing her hands on her hips, she shook her head. "You have to put on pants. I'm not sending you through the portal naked."

"Oh, come on! I want to know what it feels like. I've heard it can be a rather arousing experience. If you know what I mean?" Orion wiggled his eyebrows, his gold eyes dancing with amusement as Paisley turned bright red and started giggling so hard it sounded like she forgot how to breathe.

"Knock it off, bro," Ryker said, and hit his brother upside his head with a pair of jeans. Orion continued to laugh as he pulled the pants on and buttoned them while Aster caught Paisley staring and practically drooling at the reverse strip tease. The poor girl had it bad and was in total denial.

"Now that everyone has clothes on, let's try this again. This portal will take you right to your backyard," she said to Gage, who nodded once, giving Harlow the go-ahead. She began whispering under her breath, and the wind picked up, swirling her black hair around her face. A dark hole appeared, and the area grew while the ground beneath Aster's feet started to hum with a subtle vibration. "Okay, two at a time."

Just before Aster entered, she paused and looked over her shoulder at the campground, as if she needed further confirmation the threats that had plagued her and Gage over the past two years had truly been eliminated. Nothing had changed. The dead were still dead, and there wasn't a need to linger any longer. Satisfied, she took a step, and seconds later, Aster found herself standing in her backyard on the grass at the edge of the flagstone patio and the portal was closed behind her.

Dusk was settling in, and the solar globe string lights they had suspended from the cedar pergola had begun to glow. Through the sliding glass doors that led to the patio, Aster saw the kitchen was crowded. Reeve and Patrick were already there, huddled around Mina, who was eagerly breastfeeding. Her parents stood off to the side watching, a million emotions playing on their faces: a range of joy, excitement, and sadness.

Reeve's time with her memories was running out. There was a little over a week left before their parents, Paisley, and Harlow had to return to Havenwood Falls or risk losing their memories too. Reeve wasn't able to return, so Aster had to decide if it was worth taking a trip to Havenwood Falls to reestablish a connection with a town that tossed her and Reeve out.

CHAPTER 9

*T*he night after Mina was found and brought home, Aster pulled out the photo album and sat down in the living room with Reeve and their parents. They spent hours going through it, and Reeve and Aster slowly rediscovered their childhoods. Aster was shocked to learn that she and Reeve didn't get along and fought constantly growing up. She couldn't imagine a life without her sister. Tears fell, and there were long pauses on the pages that contained pictures of Braden. Her mom pulled out her phone and shared pictures of Braden's boy, a spitting image of his father; he'd grown considerably and was no longer the toddler Aster remembered.

Time was not on their side. With each passing day, the memory spell deadline loomed larger. Their parents had to get back to Havenwood Falls. They had a business to run, and the twins they adopted sounded like they needed some supervision. All of them were hesitant about saying goodbye when they were just getting to know each other again.

Aster rolled over and stared at Gage, who was sleeping soundly. They had the house to themselves. Her parents were staying with Patrick and Reeve. With the threat of Eben eliminated, there weren't any extra men standing guard. Everything was quiet, and still, sleep remained elusive. She sighed and rolled over again, this time to stare at the faint glimmer of stars beyond the bedroom window. The mattress shifted and then Gage was pressed up against her. His arm slid underneath hers, and his hand spanned her stomach. He kissed her bare shoulder.

"Can't sleep?" he asked.

"No." She relaxed against him.

"So do you want to talk about it?"

"About what?" she asked.

"Come on, babe. You're my mate, and we've been together for two years. I know why you're unable to sleep."

"Oh yeah, smarty pants?" She rolled over in his arms to face him, placing her palm over his tattoo. It was of his family crest, an ornamental shield with his last name, Barrows, written in fancy script at the top. "And why's that?"

"You're conflicted about going home, but you don't want to lose your parents again after just getting to know them."

Damn, he really did know her. Tears welled in her eyes, and one dripped down her face. He wiped the tear away with his thumb before cupping her cheek and placing a soft, tender kiss on her lips.

"I think you should go," he said when he ended the kiss. "Harlow and Paisley are true friends if they came all this way to help you. Your parents love you, and you need to learn more about your past. I think you'll regret it if you don't go."

"But what about Reeve? It isn't fair to her. She can never go back. I fear she'll resent me." Aster curled into his warm body. His arms wrapped around her in a comforting embrace.

"Do it for her. Be the bridge that connects you both." Her face was pressed against his chest, and his voice rumbled in her ear. "Just make me a promise . . ."

Tilting her head, she peered up at him. "What's that?"

"Come home to me. I can't live without you—you're my heart." She melted at his words and kissed his chest right above his tattoo.

"And you're mine. You couldn't keep me away. I love you, Gage Barrows."

"I love you too." Gage kissed the top of her head and held her close. It was decided, then. She was going to Havenwood Falls.

It was a tearful farewell. Aster's throat was thick with emotion as she watched Reeve hug their parents fiercely. When Aster told her sister that she was going to Havenwood Falls, she expected Reeve to be upset, yet she was surprisingly understanding. Reeve was mad about being banished but grateful that through Aster she'd have a connection to their parents, even if her memories of them faded. There weren't any rules in place that prevented Aster from bringing Mina for visits. At least her daughter could have a relationship with her grandparents. She didn't know how that would work with the memory spell, though. Her niece's memories would disappear every time she left Havenwood Falls. *One thing at a time*, she thought to herself as she closed the front door behind her.

Aster's suitcase was tucked in the trunk of her Sentra, next to her parents' bags. Since Harlow, Paisley, Orion, and Crusher had already left, she and her parents were driving back in Aster's car. Apparently, it was a six-hour drive. They would be arriving sometime in the afternoon.

"All set. I topped off the fluids." Gage closed the hood and stuck an oil-soaked rag in the back pocket of his jeans.

"This is in good shape," her dad said, tapping the roof. "We got it for you as a college graduation present."

"You did?" Aster tilted her head, and then a vague memory surfaced. "You had a big green bow on top, right?"

Her dad laughed and nodded, clearly pleased she had recovered another piece of her past. He stepped away from the car and looked over to where Reeve was talking to her mom, who was holding Mina. "I'm just going to say goodbye one more time."

"Okay, Dad." Aster watched him take Mina. She was so tiny next to his big build. His biceps alone were bigger than his granddaughter. Gage came to stand next to her, placing an arm around her waist, his hand resting on her hip. She leaned into him as they both watched the second round of tearful farewells.

"You'll call me when you get in?" he asked.

"Yes."

"And you'll call me if you need anything?"

"Of course." She almost laughed, because they had already been over this, but when she glanced up at him, his blue eyes were fixed on her and his expression was so serious. Turning to face him, she stuck her hands in his front pockets and tugged him forward. He placed his hands on her hips. "Babe, I'll miss you too."

"This will be the longest we've been apart." Gage lowered his forehead and pressed it against hers. "I feel like I'm letting a part of me go."

"I'll be back in a week." Standing on her tiptoes, she tilted her head and kissed him. She was so caught up in the moment, she forgot they were standing in the street with her parents just a few feet away until her dad cleared his throat.

Stifling a giggle, she started to pull away, breaking off the kiss. She knew her cheeks were flushed, and it felt like her lips were swollen. Tucking a stray hair behind her ear, she turned toward her parents, who were grinning like they just won the lottery.

"It's so good to see our girls with their mates," her mom said with a dreamy sigh.

"Thank you for taking care of our daughters," Aster's dad said, and he shook Patrick's and Gage's hands before giving Reeve a final hug.

Aster hugged Reeve and her sister held on tight.

"Call me and let me know how it is. Promise?" Reeve asked when she pulled away. Aster promised and slid into the passenger seat. Their next stop would be Havenwood Falls.

At first, her dad pointed out landmarks along the way and

made small talk, but as they left the highway and starting driving through the mountains, Aster grew quiet, pensive. Traffic thinned out, and they went almost half an hour without seeing another vehicle.

Her dad picked up on her silence and glanced over at her. "Nervous?"

"A little bit," Aster admitted. "I didn't exactly leave on the greatest of terms, did I?"

"It's hard to explain. The Court is responsible for governing the supes in town and has worked tirelessly to keep Havenwood Falls a sanctuary for our kind and others. The Court's decisions are harsh, but they have to be—to protect the town and its supernatural residents."

"I still don't understand."

"Shifting in public, especially in front of humans, is a major infraction. Add in the fight and the fact that there were two deaths —that required a lot of magic to cover up. The Court had to lay down the law and send a message. It wasn't personal, baby girl. You served your sentence, and there won't be any further judgment. Hopefully once you're back in town, it will make more sense." He reached across the console and placed his hand on her knee, giving it a squeeze.

"I'm just glad you decided to come home," her mom spoke up from the backseat. "Your dad and I missed you both so much."

"It's so surreal, you know?" Aster turned in her seat, making eye contact with her mom. "I feel as if there is so much more I don't know. It's been hard to wrap my head around everything."

"That's understandable. Give yourself some time."

Just then the car went around a sharp bend, and Aster felt something ripple across her skin and a brief pressure in her head, like she needed to pop her ears, but the sensation was gone within seconds.

"What was—did you feel that?" She looked at her dad, who nodded.

"We just passed through the wards that protect Havenwood Falls, which means we have twenty-five miles to go."

Aster turned her attention back to the tree-lined road. It seemed vaguely familiar, like something out of a dream. She rolled her window down and breathed in deeply, her enhanced sense of smell processing every little scent. She detected all the organic, earthy odors like damp soil and decomposing leaves. Wildflowers blooming along the side of the road sweetened the air. Deeper in the forest, she scented urine belonging to a wolf. The farther they drove, the more she picked up hints of civilization—wood smoke, grilled meat—and soon she heard the distant chatter of voices.

Minutes later they passed a sign that said *Welcome to Havenwood Falls* in black metal lettering. The base was layered stone, which blended into the natural environment. Aster leaned forward in her seat to look out the windshield, and butterflies erupted in her stomach. After curving around yet another bend and driving even higher, they crested a ridge. Her dad slowed down to stop on the side of the road so Aster could take in the town spread out below. A reddish-brown wolf seemed to materialize out of the trees on the other side of the road. The animal watched the vehicle, and her dad rolled the window down.

"It's just me, Rusty. This is Aster's car," he called to the wolf, who raised his front right paw in the air, as if to wave, before turning away and loping off into the woods. Then Aster remembered Rusty was part of the Kasun pack and patrolled the area.

Another memory surfaced of her in her mountain lion form, crouched on a ridge and staring down at the town, only it was night and the box canyon glittered like a blanket of stars. The emotions tied to that memory hit her like a punch in the gut. She had been so angry and betrayed—by Reeve. Aster gasped and placed a hand over her heart as if in physical pain. She couldn't imagine having those feelings toward Reeve.

"You're beginning to remember more, aren't you, sweetheart?" her mom asked, placing a hand on her shoulder.

"I think I'm better off not remembering."

"Oh, honey. It's not all terrible."

Aster twisted the hem of her shirt as she processed the memory, dissecting it. Apparently, she had been dating Patrick before she met Gage, and when Reeve showed up, the mating instinct kicked in. Reeve and Patrick were helpless against the instinct. Aster had been heartbroken and beyond angry. It didn't seem real. Aster had no romantic inclinations toward Patrick. He was like a brother to her. The next memory to surface was one of her telling Damian Stone where he could find Reeve and Patrick. *I did that? Damian Stone had been the root of all the problems with the purists, and I had willingly given up Reeve's location?*

"I was such an asshole. I did terrible things."

"We can all be assholes, baby girl," her dad said. "We all make mistakes. That's part of life. I do know that who you were before you left Havenwood Falls is not who you are now. You've grown up." He winked at her and smiled. Laugh lines fanned around his blue eyes, and a faint dimple appeared in his cheek. She noticed the stubble growing along his jaw had traces of gray. "Now come on, let's get home."

Driveways were the first sign of civilization, but the homes those driveways led to were shrouded by trees. They passed over a river, the water clear and sparkling in the afternoon sun. Then a development came into view on the left.

"Creekwood!" Aster blurted out, clapping her hands and bouncing with excitement in her seat like she was kid on the way to Disneyland. The golf course greens were perfectly manicured and busy. It was the day before the Fourth of July, and people were getting a jump on their long weekend. "Nothing has changed," she marveled as they drove through the familiar neighborhood.

Well some things had changed. They passed the Underwoods' house, and Paisley's younger brother, Dalton, was skateboarding down the driveway. He had grown since she last saw him. Two years and going from middle school to high school made a big difference.

When they approached the house she grew up in, a flood of memories washed over her. Birthdays and holidays, when she lost her first tooth and when she experienced her first shift, when Braden found his mate and when Jacob was born. It was too much all at once, and she didn't know whether she was going to throw up or cry. She just felt hot and panicky. Her dad had barely parked the car next to a pickup truck when Aster flung the door open and jumped out. She bent over, hands on her knees, gulping in fresh air. Then her mom was there, rubbing her back and telling her to breathe.

Once the feeling passed, Aster and her mom walked up the rest of the winding driveway to a walkway that led to the front door. Mountain irises were in full bloom and lined the walkway, filling the air with their sweet fragrance. Her parents' house was a large two-story made primarily of gray stone with wood trim and features. Large windows faced the street, and a wide wooden double door made up the front entrance. Her mom unlocked the door, and they stepped inside to a spacious entryway. A large ceiling fan circled overhead, suspended from the high ceiling. The living room was to the right, and it connected with the dining room by an arched entryway. To the left was her dad's office and straight ahead there was the staircase to the second floor. A hallway extended from the entryway past the staircase and straight back to the kitchen. The smell impacted Aster the most and resonated deep. A blend of her parents' scents and years of living concentrated under one roof. Home. This was home.

There were some new, unfamiliar scents mingled with the old, and she raised her nose in the air, sniffing. A move that clearly wasn't human. Just then, a man stepped into the hallway from the kitchen. He was tall and broad, with short brown hair. She recognized the sleeve tattoo on his right arm and remembered the day he stopped over for a family barbecue to show it off to her brother. Then another, more recent memory of Nicholas Jordan, whom she always called Jordan, since that's what Braden called him, surged forth, and her knees buckled. Nicholas rushed forward with his supernatural speed and caught her before she hit the slate floor.

"Easy, Aster," he said in a soothing voice as he guided her to the plush sofa in the living room.

"You were there. You tried to save Braden." Aster clung to Nicholas's shirt and when she saw the color fade from his cheeks and the sorrow in his blue eyes, she knew he still carried that pain with him. Nicholas was one of the EMTs on the scene the day Damian Stone almost destroyed her entire family. He and Braden had been best friends basically since birth, and Nicholas was just as devastated that he couldn't save his best friend. Aster recalled kneeling next to her brother's body and Nicholas delivering the news that he was gone.

"Oh, honey!" Her mom sat down next to her on the sofa. "Come here." Aster laid her head down on her mom's lap, and her mom started running her hands through her hair—a way her mom had of comforting her ever since she was little. Aster closed her eyes, and a tear spilled out.

"I'm sorry I couldn't save him," he said, and looked away, as if unable to meet her eyes. He swallowed hard and sat back, rubbing a hand along the nape of his neck.

"Nicholas, it's not your fault. We all know who killed him," Aster's mom said.

"Me," Aster thought, or at least she thought she did, but she must have said it out loud, because both her mom and Nicholas let out sharp gasps.

"What's wrong?" her dad asked. He had just come in through the front door with their bags and set them on the entryway floor before rushing into the living room.

"Aster thinks she's to blame for Braden's death," her mom explained.

"Baby girl." Her dad sat down on the other side, so Aster was sandwiched between her parents. He placed a hand on her back. "Damian Stone killed your brother. Not you."

"But I sent him after Reeve. Braden is dead because of my actions."

"No," Nicholas said. He stood up and started pacing in front of the fireplace. He exhaled sharply and turned to face them. "Your parents are right, Aster. I couldn't save your brother, but I didn't kill him. You acted out of emotion, but you didn't know what Damian Stone was going to do, and you didn't kill your brother. The guilt is still there, though, because we lost someone we love and we wish we could have done things differently to change that. I've struggled with this for two years. Now it's catching up to you. You were blissfully free of the grief. I don't know if the memory spell is a good thing or a bad thing."

"Right now, I'd say it's a bad thing," Aster replied.

"It does get better," her mom said, stroking a hand through Aster's hair. "The grief and pain will always be there, but it hurts less as time moves on. I see so much of Braden in his son, and that makes me smile. There's a part of him still here."

"I find comfort in knowing your brother went out fighting to protect his family," her dad added. "He was loyal until the end. If he had to choose how his life would end, he would want to die for a good reason and not something senseless. I can't think of a better reason. What Nicholas said is true. I carry guilt with me too. I arrived at the fight too late and it should have been me in your brother's place."

"Dad, no!" Aster cried out. She sat up and launched herself at her dad, enveloping him in a full-body hug. His strong arms wrapped around her. "It's not your fault." She sniffed and wiped tears off her cheeks. "I get it. We all wish the whole incident with Damian Stone didn't happen. He was a sick bastard, and the world is better off without him. You're right. Braden went out fighting. He wouldn't have wanted it any other way. He was always protecting me and Reeve, most often from ourselves."

She laughed through the tears, remembering how many times Braden broke up the petty fights she and her sister had over stupid things like My Little Ponies or clothes Aster borrowed without asking. He was the peacekeeper who loved his younger sisters equally and fiercely.

"That he was, baby girl."

Grief still clung to Aster, but she felt better having talked through Braden's death with her parents and Nicholas. They'd had time to process his loss, but to her it was still fresh. Hopefully as days passed, the pain and the guilt wouldn't weigh so heavy. She relaxed her hold on her dad and grabbed the glass of water. At the rate she was crying, she was going to get dehydrated.

"How were things with Roxy and Remy while we were gone?" her dad asked Nicholas. Aster eagerly waited for the response, grateful for the change in subject and curious about the two teenagers her parents had adopted. That explained the different scents she detected when she first walked in. The twins were cougar shifters like Nicholas's mate, Audrey, who was their half sister, and their scents were new to Aster.

"Everything has been fine. Roxy is her usual contained self, although she has been acting a little odd, like she's not telling Audrey and me something. Maybe she's dating someone and doesn't want us to know?" Nicholas shrugged.

"And Remy?"

"He's trying. I'll give him that. He's been going to summer classes, but I don't know how well he's doing. At least Principal Friske hasn't called. I take that as a good sign." Just the conversation alone was providing information about what hadn't changed in the two years she'd been gone. Mr. Friske was still principal at the high school. He was such a permanent fixture, he'd probably still be there in a hundred years.

"Where are they now?"

"Roxy is working at Coffee Haven, and Crusher took Remy to work out at Get Buffed!."

"Good. Crusher will keep him in line," her dad said. Aster imagined the hulking lion shifter, who filled a room with his size, was very successful at keeping people in line.

"Yeah, and the twins seem excited about the Fourth of July. Audrey is too. It will be their first one in Havenwood Falls."

"It will be a special one for sure," her dad said, looking at Aster and giving her a wink. "Thanks for taking care of them on such short notice."

"Not a problem. It gave Audrey some quality time with them and gave us a taste of what it will be like when we have our own kids."

Aster smiled at this. "You'll be a great dad, Jordan."

He grinned. "I'm warming Audrey up to the idea."

Her dad laughed and stood up, clapping Nicholas on the shoulder. "Hopefully she doesn't fight you like she tried to resist the mating call. Good luck, son."

Aster's mom stood up too. "Come on, let's get you settled in."

Aster followed her mom up the stairs, listening as she explained how the twins were staying in her old bedroom that she had shared with Reeve. Up here their scents were stronger. One was more dominant than the other, sweet and spicy in a way, like spring grass with a hint of pepper. The fact they were using her old bedroom didn't bother Aster, as she had lived on her own in the apartment above Coffee Haven and now lived in Denver, so it technically wasn't her room anymore.

"The twins don't like to be apart from each other, and Remy is very protective of his sister. They opted to share." Her mom paused in front of the door that led to Braden's old room. He had moved out long before Reeve and Aster did, but it would always be referred to as Braden's room. "If it bothers you staying in here, we can set up the guest room. I'm sure Nicholas and Audrey will go back to their place now that we're home."

"No, Mom, it's fine." Aster opened the door and stepped inside. Nothing had changed. The walls were still navy blue with white molding and trim around the windows and doors. The same navy, green, and cream plaid comforter covered the double bed, and Braden's scent lingered—faint, but it was there. It caused a lump to form in Aster's throat. In the corner there was a stack of framed pictures and posters that had been in her room. Next to the stack was a box overflowing with high school mementos, like Reeve's Miss Teen Havenwood Falls trophy. A light layer of dust covered everything. It didn't escape her notice that this had become a tomb of sorts—a place for her parents to keep all the belongings of the children they lost. She also noticed the hesitation her mom showed before following her into the bedroom.

"Perhaps I can change the sheets? Is it too much for you?"

Aster shook her head. "Leave them. It's okay. I feel closer to Braden in here."

Her mom crossed her arms over her chest and looked around the room, her green eyes misting over with tears. "I miss him so much, and I've missed you and your sister. I'm glad you're here and that we didn't lose you completely."

"Oh, Mom." Aster crossed the room and gave her mom a hug. At that moment, she despised the Court for the pain they caused her parents. How heartless, to rip their remaining children away after just losing their son. "I hate them! I hate that they tore apart our family."

"Aster, honey." Her mom stepped away and placed her hands on Aster's shoulders to look her straight in the eye. "Promise me you won't do anything. It's in the past, and the Court does things for a reason. Don't go poking that bear."

"But—"

"No!" Her mom shook Aster slightly. "Your dad swore to the Court he would never bring up Reeve's banishment. They were generous enough to shorten yours."

"Ha! By less than a week. That's not exactly generous." Aster spun out of her mom's grasp and strode across the room to the dresser. A framed picture of her family caught her attention, taken at a time when they were a complete unit—whole, happy, and alive. "How can you be okay with it?"

"I was never okay with it," her mom said with a sad sigh. "Just promise me you'll drop the matter? I can't lose you again."

The sadness in her mom's voice quieted Aster's rage. She

looked over her shoulder to where her mom stood by the door. "I promise."

A few minutes later, Aster was alone in the room. She had brought her suitcase up and hung up some of her clothes. She had brought a sundress in case there was anything slightly dressy she needed to attend. For the most part she lived in jeans, leggings, or shorts and was happy to keep it that way. Once she was settled in, she stretched out on the bed and called Gage.

"I fucking miss you" was how he answered the phone, and she grinned, her heart racing at the sound of his voice.

"And I fucking miss you."

"How is it going?"

Aster sighed and rolled over onto her side, facing the window that provided a view of the street. "It's been emotional. I'm remembering everything."

She filled him in as much as she could, but kept tripping over her words, and explanations became jumbled. The spell prevented her from revealing too much. Gage offered his support, and that's really all she needed.

"I wish I could be there with you."

"You have your hands full, and I'm really okay—just internal crap I need to process or unload on a therapist," she joked.

"Me too. You haven't even been gone a day, and it feels like a month."

"Same. Will you survive without me?" she teased.

"I don't know."

"Well, I'm going to go help make dinner, and tomorrow I'm going to the Fourth of July celebration. That should be interesting."

"Call me if you need me. I hate being so far away."

"I will. Love you."

"Love you too."

She ended the call and set her phone down on the bedside table. Outside, the shadows were growing longer, but it was still hours until dark. The mouthwatering smell of steak drifted in through the open windows. When she got up and went downstairs, Aster realized her dad was grilling. He and her mom were on the back deck talking to a girl with shoulder-length sandy blond hair. She wore a long-sleeved shirt with leggings even though it was eighty degrees outside. There wasn't much to her—she was so thin she looked like a strong gust of wind would blow her over. The sound of the screen door sliding open caused all heads to turn in Aster's direction. The wind blew in her direction too, and the wild peppery scent she smelled earlier washed over her. The girl with honey-colored eyes and sandy blond hair regarded Aster cautiously as she approached.

"You must be Roxy. I'm Aster." She held her hand out to the young cougar shifter, who hesitated briefly before shaking her hand with a surprisingly firm and confident grip.

"Hi." Roxy had a soft voice and shy smile. There was a wariness about her, as if she was always on alert and ready to run.

"So, you work at Coffee Haven? I used to be the manager there. How's Willow?"

"Um, she's good." Roxy looked down at the book in her hand that had a library sticker on the spine.

"Willow is the best." There was an awkward silence. Engaging in conversation with Roxy was like pulling teeth. Either the girl was painfully shy or just didn't like talking to people. "Okay, well I'm going to see if Dad needs any help. It was nice meeting you."

Roxy looked up briefly, a flash of honey eyes, and then she was gone, disappearing inside the house. Aster stared after the slip of a girl.

"She'll warm up to you, and trust me, when she has something to say, she'll say it. Roxy just isn't talkative. She's always been aloof, except with her brother," her mom said from where she was setting out bowls of food on a side table. There were chips, a pasta salad, a potato salad, and a veggie tray in addition to a tray of rolled deli meats and cheeses. This was a spread for a party.

"Uh, what's with all the food?" Aster asked.

"We're doing family dinner tonight. You have relatives who can't wait to see you!"

Stifling a groan, Aster plastered a smile on her face. She really did want to see the rest of her family, but she was exhausted. The memory surges were taking a lot out of her, and it was still only day one of being home. "How can I help?"

"There are cases of beer and wine on the counter. If you can fill up that cooler over there, that'd be great." Her mom pointed at a large white Igloo cooler that was up against the side of the house. After several trips, the white wine and beer were packed into the ice and chilling down. She brought the red wine out and set it on the table with the food. It was from Stone Falls Winery, the local vineyard and winery in town run by the Blackstone family. Aster paused for a second when she realized she knew that without even trying and without a memory surfacing. It was just general knowledge, like it had never been wiped from her mind to begin with.

Her grandparents were the first to arrive, and the moment she saw them, all her worries about being exhausted faded. She was wrapped up in a giant bear hug from her grandpa Daniel, and her cheeks were showered with kisses from her grandma Colleen. Her dad's parents were not afraid to show affection. They hadn't changed much from her last memory of them. Her grandmother's white hair was still in her signature shoulder-length style. Her grandpa was not as muscular as her dad, but close. He kept in shape, and it showed. He didn't look eighty-seven years old, but more a spry seventy.

"Aster, dear, let us get a look at you!" her grandma said, holding Aster at arm's length for inspection. "You're just as beautiful as ever!" Her brown eyes shone with emotion. "It's so good to have you home."

Aster was pulled into another enthusiastic hug, which she willingly accepted. Her grandmother always smelled like sunshine and exuded warmth.

Her mom's twin aunts and their mates showed up next and

put Aster through the same examination. By the time they had moved on to her mom, Aster's face hurt from smiling.

Great-Aunt Cordelia's husband, Great-Uncle Paul, was telling the most outrageous story from their latest trip to Las Vegas when Aster's sister-in-law showed up with Jacob walking beside her. Aster's heart just about broke when she saw her nephew and how much he had grown. He looked so much like Braden, he could have been his clone. It was remarkable and almost too much.

Jacob stopped and stared at Aster, then tilted his head and narrowed his eyes, looking at her like she was a puzzle he was trying to figure out.

"Who are you?" he blurted out.

Moving so she was kneeling in front of him, Aster held her hand out. "I'm your aunt Aster. It's so nice to meet you."

Jacob looked at her hand for a few seconds, then shrugged and shook it.

"Will you make me a s'more?" he asked.

"Jacob, not until after dinner. You know the rules," Kaitlyn, his mother, scolded.

"Yeah, but Aunt Aster might not."

His response caused Aster to laugh, and she shook her head. "I have a feeling I'd better learn them quick, before you and I both get into trouble."

From that point on, Jacob was glued to her side. He had a million and one questions about Denver and whether dinosaurs lived there. After dinner and two s'mores, he crawled up in her lap and fell asleep. She held him close and leaned down to place a kiss on top of his head, breathing in his scent when she was done.

"You're good with him," Kaitlyn said, setting a glass of white wine on the table in front of Aster before sitting down across from her with her own glass. She had put on a sweater and unclipped her hair, so it fell around her shoulders in blond waves.

"He's a good kid."

"He is, and he's a lot like his father." Kaitlyn took a sip of wine. "I really miss your brother."

"I do too."

"Are you staying?" she asked.

Aster shook her head. "I need to go back to Denver, but I'll be back to visit at least once a month. And I'm going to figure out a way to end Reeve's banishment. She needs to be here as much as me. Wait until you meet Mina."

"How are you going to do that? The Court isn't known for their flexibility."

"I don't know yet." She sipped on her wine and contemplated the problem. She had to find a way—even if it meant pleading with the assholes.

Long after dinner was over and Aster was upstairs in Braden's room, she lay awake thinking about how she could appeal to the Court. There was one detail she kept circling back to—her parents said that Michaela Petran had ruled in their favor when it came to ending Aster's sentence early. Michaela hadn't been on the Court yet when the original sentences were handed down. She and Reeve were in the same grade, and while they were competitive with one another, they got along for the most part. Aster remembered it wasn't long before she and her sister were banished that Michaela had returned to Havenwood Falls after being gone. She too had lost her memories. She'd have to feel some kind of empathy toward Reeve's situation. Would it be enough so she'd vote in the McCabes' favor?

CHAPTER 10

"*I*'m worried about Aster," Anne said, as she walked into their bedroom from the en suite bathroom. Stopping at the dresser, she took out her diamond stud earrings and placed them in the wooden jewelry box Mike had made for her for their first anniversary.

"Why? She's here, under the same roof and perfectly fine." Mike closed the book he was reading and set it on the bedside table next to his cell phone, giving his wife his full attention.

"She's so angry at the Court. I worry she's going to do something stupid." This last part was muffled when she stripped off her sundress. Anne crossed the bedroom to drop it in the hamper that was in the closet. Her panties and bra followed. Mike enjoyed the show and was disappointed when she put on a nightgown.

"Her anger is understandable, but I don't think she'll act on it."

Anne sighed when she slid into bed and turned on her side to face him. "This is Aster we're talking about. Our little firecracker has a history of reacting first and thinking later."

"Well, she is a redhead, like her mother," Mike teased, lifting Anne's hand to his mouth and kissing her fingertips. She narrowed her eyes at him, ever the catlike green slits. "Do you want me to talk to her?"

"No." She briefly pursed her lips. "I made her promise not to do anything. Let's just keep an eye on her, especially tomorrow, since Court members will be at the Independence Day Festival."

"Done. I have faith in our daughter. She's matured since she left Havenwood Falls, don't you think?" Mike reached over and smoothed Anne's hair away from her face. "She stayed with the group and didn't act impulsively. I was watching her and could tell she wanted to run to that cabin when she heard Mina cry, but she hesitated. She thought before acting."

"That's true. Seeing her and Reeve get along is great too. Do you remember how many fights we had to break up?"

"Oh Christ, the hairbrush incident." Mike groaned and dramatically rolled onto his back, which caused Anne to snort-laugh.

When Reeve was fifteen and Aster was thirteen, Reeve had purchased a new hairbrush that apparently only hairstylists used, and it was "very special." Reeve had told Aster that if she touched it, she was dead. Aster did more than touch it. She cut all the bristles off and dipped it in a mud puddle. Mike had arrived home to World War III. Once the chaos died down, silence ensued. The sisters didn't talk to each other for more than two weeks.

"Tomorrow is going to be a big day for Aster, and I'm sure an emotional one. She hasn't been in town yet. We just need to be there for her and rein her in if needed."

"You're right, as always, my mate." Mike cupped Anne's cheek and leaned forward, placing a kiss on her lips. "I'll make sure to keep an eye on her."

Anne reached up and placed her hand over his. "I don't want anything to get messed up." When she looked at him, he saw the fear in her eyes. "We just got her home."

Long after Anne fell asleep, Mike lay awake, staring at the ceiling and listening to his daughter's heartbeat in the other room. That was the hardest part after the kids were all gone: the silence.

How many nights had he lain awake like that, listening to their heartbeats, assuring him they were safe and sleeping peacefully? Then, one by one, they grew up and moved out, until silence filled the house. It had taken months for him to break the habit. When Roxy and Remy moved in, he became attuned to their heartbeats, a slightly faster rhythm, one of the few distinctions between mountain lion and cougar shifters. If Roxy did get accepted to the College for Supernatural Guardians, he'd have to adjust to hearing one less heartbeat again.

He didn't want anything to get messed up either. He'd talk with Aster in the morning, remind her of what was at stake and that approaching the Court in any way that was deemed inappropriate, disrespectful, or hostile could result in severe ramifications.

With that decided, he drifted off to sleep, only to be awakened by his cell phone ringing. The planning committee for the festival needed him and one of his scissor lifts to put up decorations. Anne was half awake when he told her what was going on. He slipped out of the house before the sun had even begun to rise, his plan of talking to Aster far from his thoughts.

CHAPTER 11

*T*he next morning promised a warm, sunny day, perfect for the Independence Day Festival, where all of the events were planned for outside. Aster woke early and made a batch of blueberry scones plus one of her new recipes for raspberry sour cream scones. Her parents' kitchen was a dream. The granite countertop was perfect for setting hot trays on, and there was plenty of counter space. Sunlight spilled in through the numerous windows, so she didn't need to turn on any lights.

Remy was the first to arrive, lured by the enticing smells. He wore cargo shorts that hung on his hips and a wrinkled McCabe & Sons T-shirt. His sandy brown hair was pulled back in a man bun, and that's when Aster noticed the sides of his head were shaved. She had only met him briefly the night before. Ryker had dropped him off, and he came out to the barbecue, piled about half a cow onto his plate, and disappeared. She spotted him later, sitting on the steps of the deck with Roxy.

"Mmmm," he said with an appreciative grunt when he bit into a blueberry scone. "These are like the ones at Coffee Haven."

"I know. That's my recipe." Aster wiped her hands on her apron.

"Really? That's cool." He devoured the last bite and reached for one of the raspberry scones. He grunted in approval again and snatched up a plate with three more scones and poured a giant cup of milk before going back up to his room. Aster shook her head. Her mom used to have a coronary whenever any of the kids brought food into their rooms. She didn't want ants or any kind of bugs invading the house. Her mom must be getting soft.

Moments later, her mom shuffled into the kitchen and beamed when she saw Aster. "Oh, honey, you have no idea what it means to see you here." She pulled Aster into a fierce hug. "I don't ever want to let you go."

Aster returned the hug, squeezing just as fiercely.

"Well, it would be kind of awkward if we were stuck together like this all the time," she teased, and her mom laughed and let go.

"You always were a smartass. Glad that hasn't changed." Her mom winked and poured a cup of coffee, cradling the mug with both hands. She was already dressed for the day, wearing denim shorts and a red V-neck T-shirt. Her auburn hair was pulled back with a barrette.

"Where's Dad?"

"There was an emergency, and the festival planning committee called him early this morning. They needed one of his scissor lifts to put up decorations. Nothing like the last minute." She rolled her eyes. "We'll catch up with him in town."

"Where's Roxy? Remy was down and raided the scones."

"She's at Coffee Haven already. You remember those days, right?"

Aster sure did. Those early mornings were brutal, especially when she was out the night before roaming the woods and hunting. Some nights Patrick kept her up late. Her face scrunched up at the memory of having sex with the man who was now her brother-in-law. She immediately lost her appetite.

Later that morning, Aster and her mom walked to town together to catch the tail end of the parade. They wove their way through the crowds of people that lined the street to watch the parade. Everything was fine until they approached the corner of

Main and Eighth Street. One block down on Eighth Street was Havenwood Village, the apartment complex where Patrick used to live and where Braden died.

Aster froze and stared down Eighth Street, not seeing the pageantry for the Fourth of July, but the street blocked off by emergency vehicles, their lights flashing as she ran past, desperate to get to her sister, whom she had sent Damian Stone to find. At that moment in time, Aster didn't know her brother had already fought to his death and her dad was next as he faced off with Damian.

"Aster, honey." Her mom's gentle touch drew her back to the present. The vision faded, replaced by crowds of happy people wearing red, white, and blue and carrying small American flags. "Are you okay?"

Aster wiped her sweaty palms on her khaki shorts, took a deep breath and nodded. "Yeah, let's go."

She marched forward and crossed the street without a second glance.

Stepping into Coffee Haven was like stepping back in time and like she had never left. The bell above the door chimed, and Roxy looked over at them, her narrow face transforming when she smiled. Paintings from local artists decorated the walls. Hanging plants with colorful blossoms were suspended above tables, adding a natural, earthy vibe. There were a few customers sitting at tables inside, but most were outside in the small seating area on the sidewalk. Aster surveyed the menu, daily specials written on the chalkboard with colorful chalk.

"Unicorn Farts? What the hell is that?" Aster snorted at the name. Only Willow could get away with that.

"Well, it's about time you got your ass down here." Aster turned to see Willow coming down the short hallway from the back of the shop, where her office was located. In her arms she held a toddler, a little girl with white-blond hair like her mother and the most captivating gold eyes. She had a cherub face, and her fair skin practically glowed, a sign of her fae genes.

"Oh, my goodness!" Aster cried out, and hugged her former boss, who was pregnant when she last saw her. "And who is this adorable creature?"

"Meet Arabella. Want to hold her?"

Aster eagerly nodded and held her hands out.

"Hi, Arabella, I'm Aster," she said as soon as the little girl was in her arms.

"Ass!" the toddler said. "Ass! Ass! Ass!" Her little fists raised in the air as she chanted. Everyone in the shop burst out laughing.

Willow tossed her long blond hair over her shoulder and grimaced. "She's approaching her terrible twos but has the vocabulary of a sailor. I blame her father. The other day she said, 'ya wee ballbag,' Scottish accent and all."

They ordered drinks, and Aster had to try the Unicorn Farts, which was more like a milkshake than coffee and had every color of the rainbow swirling on top. Willow sat with Aster and her mom so they could catch up. Their conversation was disrupted every time Willow had to chase Arabella down. The little girl wanted to meet everyone and get into everything. By the time they left, Aster's face hurt from smiling. She promised to meet Willow for lunch before she went back to Denver.

The next stop was Danzan Park, where the cookout competition was being held, hosted by Pyntz Butcher Shoppe. Aster and her mom cut down the side streets, following the smell of grilled meat. There were tables set up for arts and crafts and face painting. Vendors were selling a variety of items like pottery, artwork, jewelry, and crystals. Kids were running around with sparklers in their hands, their faces painted. Some kids were running around with turkey drumsticks that were bigger than their arms.

Aster spotted her dad talking to Nicholas's dad, standing in the shade and eating hamburgers. Ronald Jordan pulled Aster into a one-armed hug, careful to keep his plate away from her hair, and welcomed her home.

"Your folks sure missed you," he said. "Plan on sticking around?"

Aster repeated the same line she told everyone she had run across that day because they all seemed to ask the same question. While Havenwood Falls was her hometown, her home was now in Denver, but she'd be back for visits.

Just as she was leaving to grab some food, Jacob came running up, his face painted like a tiger. Kaitlyn ran up behind him, her face flushed from the heat.

"Auntie Aster, come see!" Jacob grabbed her hand and tugged on it, urging her to follow. Who was she to ignore his request? He led her through crowds to an area set up for water gun battles. Soon they were engaged in war—Jacob and Aster versus Dalton Underwood and one his friends. Aster didn't know who won, but both teams were soaked at the end, and her belly hurt from laughing.

Her clothes were still damp when she went in search of something to drink. A beer tent called her name, and she sauntered over, bumping into a tall blond elf along the way—an elf she'd crushed on when she was a freshman in high school. He had changed a lot since then—his face was more angular and he now had sleeve tattoos on both arms.

Karson Kane smiled at her. "Hey, you're Reeve's little sis, right? I heard you were back in town. It's a bummer Reeve couldn't come back. She was always fun to hang with. How's she doing?"

"Yeah, I wish she could be here, too, and she's good. She's married and has a baby."

"That's cool. Well, tell her I said hi, not that she'll remember me." With nothing else to say, Karson continued on. He wasn't the only one of Reeve's friends Aster had run into. While Reeve may have forgotten Havenwood Falls, the people certainly had not forgotten her. The old Aster would have been jealous, but the new Aster just missed her sister. Aster shook off the melancholy thought and was pleased to run into Harlow and Crusher waiting in line at the beer tent. Crusher was in full biker mode, wearing black boots, distressed jeans, and a leather vest covered in patches over a black tank top. He wasn't the only one. There were several members of the SIN MC hanging out.

"Oh my Goddess! I'm so glad you're here!" Harlow pulled Aster into a hug. "Have your memories returned?" she whispered in her ear so as to not be overheard.

"They have. It's been . . . overwhelming. Yeah, overwhelming is the best way to describe it."

"I bet. I can't even imagine."

"I know exactly what it's like," a woman said from behind Aster, who turned around to see Michaela Petran. Of course, the moroi vampire would have heard Harlow's whisper. Michaela, like most supernaturals, had enhanced senses. "Aster, welcome home. I hope all is well?"

Aster opened her mouth, preparing to give the Court member an earful, to tell her off for their shitty rules and decisions, but then she remembered that Michaela could be an ally.

"I'm adjusting," she said instead.

"Good. I saw you over here and wanted to check in. Just take it one day at a time—that's what I did. And if you ever want to talk, stop by the inn. I'm usually there." Michaela owned Whisper Falls Inn, which had been in the Petran family since the beginning of the town.

"Okay. I'll keep that in mind." Aster watched her walk away to join Addie Beaumont, who was standing by the table for the poultry cook-off. There were stations set up for the cook-off, one for each meat variety.

"Wow," Harlow said, handing Aster a beer. "That was cool of her. Come on, let me introduce you to some of the guys."

Aster was pulled into a sea of bikers. That night, after the dance, Aster fell into bed completely exhausted. She rolled over, wanting to tell Gage about her day, then remembered he wasn't there. The next time she visited, she was bringing him. She drifted off to sleep thinking of her mate, longing to be by his side.

In the morning, it was just Aster and her parents sitting

around the table on the deck drinking coffee. McCabe & Sons was closed until Monday, giving the employees and owners some time off. Since it was just the three of them, Aster decided to broach the subject of appealing Reeve's banishment.

"How do I go about doing it?"

Her dad shook his head, his mouth set in a grim line. "I don't think you'll be successful, baby girl. They seemed pretty adamant about her sentence remaining in place when we asked for yours to be shortened. In fact, I promised not to bring it up."

She scowled at his response because it wasn't what she wanted to hear. Determined, she leaned forward, placing her elbows on the table. "What if I present it as a benefit to the town? I know I tend to make decisions based on emotion, but that isn't going to work here. Asking for Reeve's banishment to end because we miss her isn't a good enough reason. It will be a waste of time."

"Agreed. So what are you thinking?" her dad asked.

"I'm thinking about proposing an alliance between the Denver den and Havenwood Falls. In the short time I've been here, I've heard other supes talking about several incidents involving outside threats. Damian's attack is just one example. Reeve was threatened, and she ran to the one place she thought would protect her. Harlow told me how the alliance between the witches and witch hunters here is unique. Then there's this Collector? If the Collector is targeting supes, isn't that a concern for supes everywhere—not just Havenwood Falls? They've expanded Sun and Moon Academy to train a supernatural army, and it's not just to protect Havenwood Falls but the world. An alliance with another den will help communicate these threats and share information. Or if the need arises, we can fight for each other. The fact that you're the alpha and your daughters are mates to the alpha and beta of the Denver den means the alliance will be built on family, trust, and loyalty."

Her dad grinned at her, laugh lines crinkling around his blue eyes. "You've really thought about this."

"I have. What do you think?" Aster raised her mug to her lips and took a sip of coffee, her eyes moving from her dad to her mom to get a read on their reactions.

"No," her mom said, at the same time her dad said, "Okay."

"Why not?" Aster challenged her mom.

"Because your father made a promise."

"Dad did, but I didn't!" Aster's ponytail swung from side to side as she stood suddenly, unable to sit still. She crossed over to the deck railing and leaned against it to stare out at the backyard.

"She has a point, Anne. It won't be us asking."

"But what if it backfires?"

Aster turned to face her parents. "I have to try. I'll regret it forever if I don't."

Her mom sighed and shook her head. "All right. I don't like it, but I understand."

Her dad drummed his hands on the table and stood up. "I'm going to go make a call." He went inside the house, and Aster looked over at her mom.

"Who is he calling?" she asked, returning to her chair.

"Most likely Elsmed Fairchild. That's who he called last time to set up a hearing with the Court."

A few minutes later, her dad returned, and he sat down heavily in his chair. He took a sip of coffee and leaned back, to survey the trees overhead, drawing out the suspense.

"Dad!" Aster kicked his leg under the table after losing her patience. He jumped and rubbed his shin, feigning injury.

"You're on, kiddo. Tuesday night you can appeal to the Court. I floated your proposal by Elsmed, and he said it has some merit."

The next five days felt like an eternity. Finally, Tuesday night arrived, and Aster sat between her parents at a table that faced a prominent wooden dais. With her memory restored, she knew exactly who everyone was, and the anxiety from her last hearing resurfaced. Elsmed still creeped her out with his glacial stare.

Harlow's grandmother smiled briefly at them before returning to an all-business expression. Lawrence Mills looked like something had crawled up his butt. Michaela Petran was on the end closest to Addie Beaumont, and they were having a side conversation. Roman Bishop looked like he had better things to do and leaned back in his chair, assuming the pose of a bored teenager in class.

Mayor Barbie Stuart rapped the gavel, calling the meeting to order and ending the murmur of voices. "Aster, welcome home. I'm sure the rules were explained to you?"

"Yes."

"Good. Mike, I understand everything went well and you found your granddaughter?"

"That's correct. She's safe."

"How was it working with the Denver den?" Elsmed asked.

"It went really well. No issues. Gage, Aster's mate, is very capable."

"Good to hear. You never know when a future alliance will be needed." Elsmed winked at Aster, surprising her with his candidness. "And the threat has been eliminated?"

"Yes."

"Excellent. Now, Aster, I understand you want to appeal your sister's banishment as well as her mate's?" Elsmed didn't waste any time getting down to business.

There were rumblings among the Court, and Lawrence Mills shifted angrily in his seat, muttering something that sounded like "no respect for the rule of law."

"Michael McCabe, not even a month ago you sat in that very chair and said you had no plans of appealing Reeve's sentence," Saundra Beaumont said.

"I remember, Saundra, and I'm not. Aster is appealing. Anne and I are here for emotional support. Go ahead, baby girl." Her dad patted the top of her hands, which were tightly clenched on the table before her. It was going to take a crowbar to pry them loose.

Aster took a deep breath and stood, her chair screeching on the floor when it moved back, making her jump. Her stomach was a jumble of nerves as she approached the Court. She felt so insignificant with them looming over her. The last time she was here, they had cast her out without a second thought. She took another deep breath to settle the fear and anger she felt rising. Now wasn't the time to lose her temper.

She had dressed for the occasion. She knew her casual attire wouldn't fly with this crowd steeped in formality and tradition. Aster had chosen a black pencil skirt and an emerald green silk tank top. Instead of sneakers or flip-flops, she wore black heels that boosted her stature by three inches. All three items were purchased at Callie's Consignments earlier that day. She had taken time to style her hair, which hung in loose waves almost to the small of her back, where drops of sweat were beginning to collect. Unclenching her hands, she smoothed her skirt, drying her sweaty palms off on the fabric in the process.

"Members of the Court, thank you for your time this evening," she began, and dipped her head as a sign of respect, laying it on thick to work the odds in her favor. Then she raised her head and made eye contact, keeping her spine and shoulders straight. Speaking as a true mate of an alpha and daughter of an alpha, she proposed an alliance, pointing out it was a suggestion Elsmed had already made. When she felt her emotions rising, she stopped and took a breath, reining them in. This had to be an appeal out of logic, not emotion.

When she was done, her knees were trembling and she thought she was going to throw up.

"Thank you, Aster. You and your parents may step outside. We have a lot to discuss," Saundra said.

If the wait for the hearing was an eternity, the wait for their decision was even longer. Aster paced outside in the small reception area that looked like any other municipal office in City Hall. Her heels made a steady click-clack rhythm on the linoleum floor. She chewed on a nail that had chipped at some point, most likely when her hands were clenched into fists.

"Relax, honey," her mom said. "You did amazing in there. I'm so proud of you!"

"Your mom and I both are, baby girl."

A click of the door opening caused her to jump, and she spun around. Addie Beaumont appeared. "They're ready for you."

Her parents stood up and started moving, but Aster remained rooted to the floor. What if she'd failed to persuade them? Sure, she could be a bridge between Havenwood Falls and Denver, but it wasn't the same as having Reeve experience the comfort and joy of being home, of remembering their childhood, the good and bad. Then her parents were there, one on each side, guiding her forward. They walked into the courtroom a united front and sat down at the table. Her dad held her left hand in his, and her mom held her right hand. She grasped them tightly.

"Ms. McCabe," Lawrence Mills began. "Ordinarily I would have opposed your proposal. I'm of the belief that a sentence should never be rescinded. However, you brought up some valid points. I've lived in Havenwood Falls a long time and will die to protect this town. Recent events have made me realize that might happen sooner rather than later. An alliance with others outside of our wards has become a necessity."

Aster sat there dumbfounded. Of all the Court members, she thought for sure she'd never sway Lawrence Mills.

Next, Mathilde Augustine spoke. "Damian Stone's mindset was not unique. Each species has members who think sticking with their own kind is best. I, too, have had similar thoughts, but Harlow recently taught me I was wrong. There is strength in diversity, as there is strength in numbers. Having allies outside of town that we can call on for help in a time of need will be a benefit to Havenwood Falls. This is a matter of great importance we're working on now by creating the new academy. Your family has proven themselves loyal since your grandfather settled here in 1957. Knowing you and your sister will be outside of our wards yet still have our town's best interests in mind is a comfort."

Aster squeezed her parents' hands. This was going better than she could possibly have imagined.

Michaela Petran cleared her throat, and her unique gray-green eyes settled on Aster. "As you know, I've gone through something similar, where I had forgotten my time growing up in Havenwood Falls. Now that I'm back, I know how valuable those memories are —even if they hurt. I wasn't on the Court when Damian Stone followed Reeve and when all hell broke loose. I was dealing with my own issues back then. I've reviewed Addie's notes from this incident and the minutes from the hearing. Had I been here to cast my vote, I never would have banished either you or your sister. Reeve was coming here for help. Unfortunately, what she was running away from followed her. You and Reeve weren't villains. You were victims. We should have responded faster when he came through the wards. Everything happened too fast. He's not the only threat to have done this, and each breach allows us to strengthen our defenses."

"Are we done with the speeches?" Roman Bishop interjected, and Michaela glared at him. "I'm sure I'm not the only one with plans tonight." He ran a hand over his perfectly coiffed hair. There were a few ayes and nods. "Good. Saundra, please read the Court's decision."

Oh my God, I'm really going to throw up. Aster willed her stomach to behave.

Saundra looked straight at Aster and said the words she least expected to hear. "Effective today, Reeve McCabe and Patrick O'Shea are no longer banished. We will set terms of an alliance with Gage Barrows and Mike McCabe at a later date."

"Court dismissed," Mayor Stuart declared with a rap of the gavel. The mural behind the dais hid a secret doorway that slid open. The members stood up and filed out.

"You did it, baby girl!" Her dad picked her up and spun her around, kissing her on the cheek before setting her down, where her mom engulfed her in a hug. Aster was still stunned as they walked out together. As soon as they were in her dad's truck, she pulled her phone from her bag. It was time to call Reeve—to tell her she could come home.

We hope you enjoyed this story in the Havenwood Falls series featuring a variety of supernatural creatures. The series is a collaborative effort by multiple authors.

You might also enjoy E.J.'s other stories in the Havenwood Falls universe:
Fate, Love & Loyalty (Main Series)
Fata Morgana (Havenwood Falls High)
Fated Beginnings (Legends of Havenwood Falls)
Stray With Me (Sin & Silk)
Havenwood Falls Short Story Anthology 2018
Sun & Moon Academy Book One: Fall Semester
Sun & Moon Academy Book Two: Spring Semester

Also look for the YA line, Havenwood Falls High; the historical paranormal line, Legends of Havenwood Falls; the sexier side of town, Havenwood Falls Sin & Silk; the local supernatural college, Sun & Moon Academy; and the Havenwood Falls holiday short story anthologies.

Stay up to date at www.HavenwoodFalls.com

E.J. FECHENDA

ABOUT THE AUTHOR

E.J. Fechenda has lived in Philadelphia and Phoenix, and now calls Portland, Maine, home. She is the Amazon bestselling author of the New Mafia Trilogy and in addition to working on the Ghost Stories Trilogy, she's a contributing author for the Havenwood Falls series. She has a degree in Journalism from Temple University, and her short stories have been published in *Suspense Magazine* and several anthologies.

You can find her on the internet here:

Facebook: https://www.facebook.com/EJFechendaAuthor

Twitter @ebusjaneus (https://twitter.com/ebusjaneus)

Tumblr: http://ejfechenda.tumblr.com/

Bookbub: https://www.bookbub.com/authors/e-j-fechenda

ACKNOWLEDGMENTS

This was a particularly challenging story to write, since it's been two years since I wrote *Fate, Love & Loyalty*. A lot has happened in Havenwood Falls, and with the McCabe family, since then. There were some last-minute adjustments with the timeline or with shared characters, but every single author I collaborated with and called on for help at the eleventh hour made themselves available without complaint. Amy Hale, Randi Cooley Wilson, Morgan Wylie, Kristie Cook, Susan Burdorf, and C.J. Pinard, thank you for letting me use your characters. A special big shout-out goes to Victoria Escobar—thank you, dear friend, for those late night brainstorming sessions about the differences between mountain lions and cougars. Thank you for giving me some creative license with Roxy and Remy. Mike and Anne hope they're happy in their home. Liz Ferry, with Per Se Editing, I have dubbed you "Eagle Eye"—thank you for your attention to detail.

This story was written with the support of family, friends, caffeine, chocolate, wine, and during particularly manic writing sessions, lots of salty snacks. I see the need for a treadmill desk in my near future.

AN EXCERPT

~ A Havenwood Falls New Adult Novella ~

HAVENWOOD FALLS

FATE'S DEMAND

EMILY CYR

Fate's Demand (A Havenwood Falls Novella) by Emily Cyr

She's been the oracle for less than a month and she's already angered the gods. If she doesn't meet fate's demand, all of Havenwood Falls will suffer.

Lana Velis always knew she might one day inherit the powers and duties of the Oracle of Delphi, but the inheritance arriving in the middle of her last-ever college final wasn't something even she could predict.

With a power she never wanted and her testy cat, Lana must leave her best friend behind and make her way to Havenwood Falls to take over the never-ending petitioner list her ya-ya left behind. If only it were that easy. Now, not only is she saddled with a guardian she has no interest in having, but she's also forced to live with him.

And the hurdles keep coming. First, Lana must convince the Court of the Sun and the Moon to honor her title as the sacred oracle. Then she's bound by the laws of the gods to never tell someone's future if they aren't on her list—a law she struggles with, especially when she sees the unfathomable future of a little boy.

Now the gods are angry, and the Fates demand a soul in place of the one she stole—or all of Havenwood Falls will suffer the consequences. Lana must choose a soul to sacrifice, because in the end, Fate will always get its due.

FATE'S DEMAND

BY EMILY CYR

The way her short silver hair kissed that slim neck of hers sent chills throughout my whole body. That neck I'd spent two years loving, spent two years brushing my lips against. Now? Just what was I supposed to do? I was expected to just pick up the remnants of my shattered heart and move the hell on. How could anyone be expected to do that?

She knew I was there. I could tell by the way she hung all over the other woman. The one I'd caught her with. I was so stupid for still loving her, but apparently, she'd moved on long ago.

"Lana. You can't keep doing this to yourself." It was Jensen chiding me. It was always Jensen. Her kind voice had always been a balm to my soul, ever since we were kids. Now, here we were only a few finals until we graduated from college. She with a degree in education and I in graphic design. But as it was, none of that mattered, not when my heart had been so viciously ripped out.

"Earth to Lana," she prodded again. This time I glanced at her. She looked so much like the child she used to be, I couldn't help but smile at her. Her light brown skin was such a contrast to her vivid green eyes. Her spiraled ringlet curls hung around her face, making her rounded features stand out even more. She was beautiful. I was always so jealous of her. She stood at a whopping five foot seven, whereas I was five foot two on a good day. My skin seemed so pale in comparison to her richly tanned color, even though my Greek heritage gave me an olive complexion. However, she always said I never appreciated my pin-straight dark brown hair. She was right, as usual. My eyes were always my favorite feature. They were a bright blue and against my dark hair they stood out even more.

I sighed. "I know, it's just, I—" I choked on the words.

Jensen held up a slender hand in a stopping gesture. Her brow and lips tilted up slightly, causing her features to soften slightly. "I know you do. But you deserve better, girl."

Of course, she was right. "I know." There wasn't a whole lot more I could say.

"Come on, we have a final to get to. Did you even study? Greek history—shouldn't you be an expert? You being Greek and all?"

Glancing down at my phone, I realized she was correct. It was the only class the three of us shared, so it wasn't like it would be awkward or anything.

"Fuck no!" I exclaimed. I tried like hell to recall the last semester's worth of Greek history. "What were the three Fates' names again?" I blurted.

"Girl, if I have to tell you that, you're totally screwed." She laughed, shaking her head.

We walked to class as we always did, her trying to make me laugh, me brooding while trying like hell to remember the Fates' names and everything else I needed for that damn exam.

"So, what? Are you going to go back to dudes now?"

Her question caused me to choke on my own saliva.

Half coughing and half laughing, I looked at her and explained, "That's not really how it works. I'm bi. I kinda just love who I love."

"I know it's not, but I heard a laugh or two around that cock you were choking on just now, so hashtag worth it." Her crazy ass seemed to preen as her face lit up.

"You're the most inappropriate person I know." I laughed, rolling my eyes at her.

"Oh, that's so not true. You've met my mother."

"You win!" I cackled as we rounded the corner and walked into class.

This was it. My last final I'd have to take before real life would come crashing down on me.

We made our way to our seats and got settled in. My phone buzzed, and I looked down to see the text.

It was from my dad. Like I'd done for the last five years, I hit ignore. The absolute last thing I needed right then was my alcoholic father hitting me up for yet more money.

"Let me guess, your dad or ya-ya? Still letting them walk all over you?" It was her. My whole body froze at her words, not because of what she said but because of who had said it.

"Don't you have a rock to find, Cassidy?" Jensen taunted in a venom-laced tone.

Cassie looked at her in confusion.

"What?" Cassie spat. Her eyes were laser focused on Jensen.

"Oh, you know, the rock you crawled out from under and need to return to?" I heard several shocked inhalations of breath from around me at Jensen's dig.

I swear to Hades's bouncing balls my jaw hit the fucking tile floor with an audible clack.

The look of shock and hurt flashed so fast across Cassie's face, I questioned if I'd seen anything at all.

"See, this is why I found something better. You're no better than the company you keep. Remember that, Lana." She was so condescending. Come to think of it, she'd always been like that, not just to Jensen but to me as well. And her words were nothing more than a slap in the face meant to hurt me and Jensen. Then, under her breath, she said the words I thought I would never hear from someone I'd once loved: "No wonder your dad's an alcoholic."

I was so shocked I just sat there for a heartbeat. Then rage took over, and I stood to face her eye to eye. I'd had enough. Not because I actually cared about my father, but for the sheer fact that she had the gall to blame me for something I'd always blamed myself for—something she'd known. She had the audacity to use my own insecurities against me? Yeah, fuck that.

"You know, Cassie, as I recall, I broke up with you. And, as I recall, you were trying to sext me, what, just last night? So really, who's the lucky one?"

She opened her mouth to speak, but fuck that. I wasn't having it.

"So, you want to give me advice?" I continued. "How about I give you some? You are what you eat."

The whole class was listening, including the TA and professor. I should have cared about the audience. But for once, I didn't care whom I offended or who heard my dirty laundry.

"What?" she said dumbly. Looking around for a split second, I saw the same look on nearly everyone's face.

Smiling my very best *eat shit and die* expression, I intoned, "You are what you eat. Me? I last ate a bagel. What did you eat? A rotting, stinking pus—" The world tilted and went black. But not before I saw Cassie's horrified expression. I couldn't help but laugh. Well, at least I thought I did.

Purchase *Fate's Demand* where books are sold.

www.ingramcontent.com/pod-product-compliance
Lightning Source LLC
Chambersburg PA
CBHW052003170626
46808CB00007B/2761